Visit us at www.boldstrokesbooks.com

MISSING

By the Author

From This Moment On

True Confessions

Missing

MISSING

by
PJ Trebelhorn

2012

MISSING

ISBN 10: 1-60282-668-4
ISBN 13: 978-1-60282-668-7

This Trade Paperback Original Is Published By
Bold Strokes Books, Inc.
P.O. Box 249
Valley Falls, NY 12185

First Edition: June 2012

Credits
Editors: Victoria Oldham and Shelley Thrasher
Production Design: Susan Ramundo
Cover Design By Sheri (graphicartist2020@hotmail.com)

Acknowledgments

I want to thank everyone at Bold Strokes Books for making my dream a reality, especially Len Barot for taking a chance on me. I'll be forever grateful.

Thanks to my editor, Victoria Oldham, for drastically improving my original draft. And to Shelley Thrasher for her expertise in cleaning it up and making it even better.

Thanks to Carsen Taite for her legal advice—it was very much appreciated even though the information you dug up didn't make it into the final version.

Thanks once again to Sheri for another awesome cover. You rock!

And I want to thank my sister Carol—your support and encouragement mean more to me than you could ever imagine.

Dedication

To Cheryl
For trying every day to make sure
there's nothing missing from my life

CHAPTER ONE

He crouched in the foliage that surrounded the playground, his knees protesting the long hours he'd spent like that. Wiping his sweaty palms on the legs of his jeans, he pulled his gloves on, thinking about the person who had given him a choice: his, and his mother's, slow deaths or abducting children whenever they told him to. He didn't know their reasons, and he didn't ask, but he was plagued with nightmares about what might be happening to the kids once he handed them over to someone else. He closed his eyes momentarily to clear his mind and tried hard to concentrate on the task at hand.

His own stupidity had gotten him into his current situation. His *addiction*. More than anything, he wished he could go to the police and let them know what he was being forced to do, but he didn't trust them—and with good reason. He couldn't even tell his mother what was happening. Because of him, her life was in danger as well. And now she was afraid of him, which broke his heart.

Silently, he watched a small boy playing alone on the jungle gym and shook his head in disgust. How unbelievable that some parents would let their kids loose in playgrounds like the one they were in.

"It could never happen to *my* kid," he muttered under his breath in a mocking tone.

This particular park had no fence to keep the kids in—or the predators out. He tried to suppress the shiver that ran down his spine at the realization that *he* was now one of those predators. He shook his head. He wasn't a molester. He'd kill himself before that would ever happen. He focused on the perimeter of the park, taking note of two women talking, but no one was paying attention to any of the children.

The boy he'd targeted looked about five years old, with blond hair and blue eyes. He fit exactly the description he'd been given, and he patted himself on the back while at the same time cursing his bad luck at having found the perfect target. The longer it took to find the perfect kid, the longer he could put off having to abduct someone. He'd thought it might get easier after the first one, but it hadn't. The little boy he was looking at was the fifth kid he'd been forced to abduct, and after having to kill the last two, he was too far in to ever realistically hope he could get out again.

The boy was only a few feet away from him, but he couldn't call him over. Too many kids nowadays were taught to scream when a stranger approached them, and he wasn't about to risk being caught.

Trying to keep his noise at a minimum, he reached behind him and pulled a golden-retriever puppy out of his backpack. After attaching some fishing line to the collar he'd put on the little beast, he set it on the ground near the tree line.

"Okay, boy, let's go fishing." He pushed gently on the puppy's backside and smiled nervously while it walked away, sniffing the ground. He waited, his pulse hammering, for the boy to notice the puppy. The gloves he slipped on kept the fishing line from cutting into his flesh, and the line itself was nearly invisible, meaning the boy would never be able to see it. The boy would think the puppy was lost and follow it back to the trees when he pulled the pup back to him. Luring the kids to him had proved to be easy, because kids seemed to be eternally enamored with puppies. Unfortunately, he was learning that abducting children was rather simple, puppy or not.

He grew even more agitated when the puppy seemed to be more interested in sniffing the trees than in getting the boy's attention. The boy finally looked over, and a huge smile broke out on his cherubic face.

"That's it…follow the puppy," he murmured shakily under his breath. He began to slowly pull the animal back to him, and the kid moved closer with each passing second.

"Hi, puppy," the boy said quietly, with a look of awe as he came along after it. The puppy kept trying to turn around and look at the boy, wagging its tail, but he kept tugging the line, slow and steady. When the boy finally crossed the tree line, he quickly removed his gloves. The blood pounding loudly in his ears, he clumsily threw the gloves into his backpack, cut the line from the dog's collar, and tossed the bag over his shoulder before he picked the puppy up. He attempted to smile warmly at the kid while shoving the small knife into his pocket. There was no going back now.

"Hi, there. Thanks for finding my dog." He scratched the pup's head and could see the boy beginning to panic. It was time to try to put him at ease, which was the hardest part. "What's your name?"

"Timmy," the boy said shyly. He looked over his shoulder, apparently searching for his mother, but they were far enough into the trees that she wouldn't be able to see them.

"Hi, Timmy. My name is Mark, and this little guy here is Sparky. I've got a few more just like him at home. Would you like to see them?" He smiled when Timmy nodded excitedly. "Hey, maybe you can even take one home with you. Would you like that?"

"It's my birthday!" Timmy clapped his hands together and nodded again.

"Is it? That's great. How old are you?" Timmy held up his hand, displaying five fingers. *Perfect.* He had been walking backward slowly, and Timmy was coming along with him, just as he knew he would. It was all too easy. "Wow, you're a big boy, aren't you? Can I give you a puppy for your birthday? Would your mom be okay with that?"

"Yes." His eyes were wide, and he kept looking at Sparky, who was panting and wiggling to get free.

Mark stopped and set Sparky down as he fished a leash from his backpack. After attaching it to the pup's collar, he held it out to Timmy, who immediately took it.

"Be careful now, because he likes to pull. Don't let him get away from you, all right?" Timmy nodded again, seeming to concentrate on the task Mark had given him. They were on the other side of the park, and his car was a couple of blocks away. The short walk would be the most nerve-wracking part. If someone saw them and became suspicious, or if the boy's mother suddenly realized she couldn't see him anymore, everything could fall apart. He looked down at Timmy and held his hand out. "Take my hand, because we have to cross the street. My car is just down the street a little bit."

"I'm not s'posed to go with strangers." He shook his head and refused the hand offered him.

"I'm not really a stranger though, am I?" Mark began to panic. In his mind's eye, he saw the kid screaming for help. His pulse spiked as he worked to reassure the boy. "I'm going to give you a puppy for your birthday."

"My mom'll be mad." The boy's tone indicated he was giving in, and Mark smiled in relief.

"We'll be back before she even knows you're gone, I promise." Mark took Timmy's hand, and they started quickly across the street. As long as the kid was quiet and didn't draw attention to them, anybody who saw them would simply think he was out for a stroll with his son and puppy.

They were only about twenty minutes northeast of Allentown, but as Mark quickly glanced at the surrounding streets he realized exactly how small—and isolated—the little town was. He hoped it wasn't one of those places where everyone knew everybody else's business. He pulled the hood of his sweatshirt up over his head and focused on the path ahead of him.

CHAPTER TWO

Olivia's step faltered when she emerged from the elevator and saw the young woman sitting on the floor outside her apartment. No, not a woman at all, but at thirteen, Kim Walters looked the part. Liv shifted the weight of her duffel bag from her shoulder to her left hand while reaching into her pocket to retrieve her keys with her right.

"What are you doing sitting out in the hall?" Liv asked when Kim glanced up at her.

"Mary took the twins to their chemo appointments." Kim shrugged indifferently and returned her attention to the iPod in her hands. "I forgot to take a key when I went to school this morning."

"Come on inside." Liv set the duffel bag down inside the door and waited until Kim entered the apartment. She motioned for the girl to have a seat at the dining-room table and went to get sodas from the fridge for both of them. "It's a little early for you to be done with school for the day, isn't it?"

"I left after lunch," Kim said, not bothering to look up from her iPod while she opened her can of soda and took a drink. "I didn't feel well."

Liv felt sorry for Kim, who had been in foster care since she was a baby. Her life mirrored Liv's early years, which cemented their bond. Liv had been a lonely teenager, pin-balling from home to home and never really feeling as if she belonged anywhere. She knew Kim felt the same way, but Kim had been with her current foster parent, Mary Farris, for almost a year. Mary wasn't someone Liv would really call a friend, but she was a neighbor Liv had come to like, and when Mary began to have trouble with Kim, she'd asked for Liv's help.

"Did the nurse send you home, or did you just leave on your own?"

"What does it matter?" Kim finally looked at her, and Liv saw the defiance in her eyes.

"It matters because you need to go to school. You've skipped out too many times recently, and if you continue, you might get taken away from Mary. Is that what you want? To be sent to some other family?" Liv watched Kim's face for any sign that she understood what Liv was telling her. "Aren't Brad and the twins enough for Mary to deal with? She's doing the best she can. Why do you insist on making things harder for her than they need to be?"

Kim shrugged, which was her usual response.

Liv sighed audibly, not bothering to hide her irritation. She knew Kim didn't love Mary, but she did *like* her, which was a huge step up from other situations she'd been in. Liv would hate to see her throw that away.

"Mary cares about you, Kim. I'd have given anything to have someone care about me when I was your age. The foster system is definitely a rough place, but there are some good people out there and Mary's definitely one of them." Liv placed her elbows on the table and tried to tell herself she wasn't nearly as tired as she felt.

"So are you," Kim said quietly. Her eyes lit up and she sat a bit straighter in her chair. "Why can't I live here with you? You said it yourself—Mary has so much to worry about with the twins, and with Brad's problems."

"We've been through this before, Kim." Liv covered Kim's hand with her own, waiting patiently for Kim to look at her. She hated destroying the girl's hopes, but they'd been having this conversation too often lately. "I'm an FBI agent. I spend long stretches of time away from home. I'm single, so nobody would be here to care for you while I'm away. You can't live with me, but you know you can come to me any time, right?"

Kim shrugged and looked toward the living room without answering. Liv sighed. Kim was obviously trying hard not to cry. She would have liked nothing more than to give Kim the stability she so desperately needed, but her lifestyle couldn't include a teenager.

"Does Emily know you consider yourself single?"

"Excuse me?" Liv pulled her hand away and sat up straighter. Kim knew Liv was a lesbian, because Liv had decided early on she wasn't going to keep the fact from her. Mary was okay with that decision, because she sensed Kim might be gay too, and she hoped Liv could help her navigate the turbulent waters of adolescence.

"Emily likes to tell me the two of you are planning to move in together, and then there wouldn't be any place for me." Kim continued to look out toward the living room, refusing to meet Liv's eyes.

"Sometimes I really wonder what Emily hears when I talk," Liv said under her breath, trying to tamp down the anger swelling inside her. She kneeled in front of Kim, waiting until Kim had looked at everything in sight before finally meeting her eyes. "You listen to me, all right? Emily is *not* moving in with me. She and I don't get along nearly well enough to live together. If she *ever* says anything to you about it again, I want you to come straight to me. I don't want any misunderstandings between us because of something someone else tells you, okay?"

Kim nodded before lowering her eyes to her lap. Liv stood again and went to the window with its glorious view of the parking lot below. She clenched her fists and silently swore to set Em straight the next time she saw her.

"Can I have the key to our apartment so I can go home?" Kim asked.

Liv wasn't surprised at the abrupt change of subject. Kim was as uncomfortable discussing personal matters as she was. Liv removed the key from her ring while Kim stood at the kitchen counter, her back to her.

"Hey," Liv said, placing a hand on Kim's shoulder and urging her to turn around. Kim turned, but kept her eyes down. Liv put two fingers under her chin and forced her to look at her. "You know, you can play the part of the tough bad-ass all you want, but I've been there, remember? I know what you're feeling, and I know how hard it is when you feel like you don't belong. You know I care about you, but I can't offer the home life you need right now. I really wish I could."

She put the key in Kim's hand.

"Are we still going to the Phillies game tomorrow?"

"You bet." Liv smiled at the hopeful look on her face. Liv had adopted the Phillies as her team when she'd moved to Philadelphia a few years earlier. The Chicago Cubs were her hometown team though, and she'd always hold a place for them in her heart. Some of the fondest memories of her childhood had taken place at Wrigley Field, and she wanted to pass a little of that pleasure along to Kim. "I've been looking forward to it since they blew the pennant last year."

"Cool." Kim gave her a tentative smile. "I'll bring the key back in a few minutes."

"No hurry. I'm planning to take a nice long nap. I'll get it from you later."

After Kim left, Liv looked across the living room at one of only two pictures on the fireplace mantle. She walked over and stopped in front of the photo, smiling at the memories it evoked. It showed her and Cindy Watt, when they were about ten years old. Cindy had been Liv's only childhood friend. From the time Liv was nine, until just after her thirteenth birthday, she and Cindy had lived with the same foster family.

Things were never easy in the system, but Liv had thought she'd found the perfect family until the Calhouns had thrown them both out after they'd been caught shoplifting. For Cindy, it had been the latest in a string of missteps, but it had been Liv's first time in trouble. That hadn't seemed to matter to the Calhouns though. They'd washed their hands of both girls and they were split up.

Liv had grown up a quiet, introverted child, believing that if she kept to herself, she wouldn't have any problems. Her anger issues started at eight years old, when she found out her mother had died of a forced overdose and her father received life without parole for her murder. Liv had gone from family to family from the age of eight months until she turned fifteen, when she finally found the right family. She turned her attention to the other photo.

Janet Andrews and her husband Kyle had been a godsend for Liv when she'd started to seriously worry she'd have no other choice but to live on the streets at eighteen. She hadn't made it easy for them to get to know her, but they'd taken her in, adopted her, and paid her way through community college to get her degree in criminal justice. They'd been there for her every step of the way since then, but at thirty-eight years old, Liv knew she could never have invented a better family for herself.

Cindy hadn't been so lucky. After the Calhouns kicked them out, she'd gone through six other families before being discharged from the system at eighteen. She'd fallen in with a bad crowd and ended up serving time for armed robbery. After that she'd been in and out of prison, and Liv had deliberately distanced herself, even though it hurt. FBI agents and lifelong criminals didn't mix well. Liv knew that, but every time Cindy got out of jail she always seemed to call Liv first. Now she was serving time for murder in Chicago, where they'd grown up, so Liv knew she wouldn't be hearing from Cindy again for a long time, if ever.

She closed her eyes and thanked the powers that be she had taken a different path than Cindy's. It would have been so easy. She held onto the picture to remind herself of a happy time in an otherwise turbulent childhood, as well as the fact that Cindy had been an innocent child at one time instead of the hardened criminal she was now. She shook her head and turned away from the mantel.

A quick glance at her watch told her it was almost two thirty in the afternoon. Without bothering to move the duffel she'd left inside the front door, she went down the hall to her bedroom, hoping to sleep straight through to the next day.

CHAPTER THREE

L iv woke to the feeling of a soft, warm hand underneath her T-shirt, working its way up to her breasts. She groaned and pressed her backside into the warm and very naked body lying behind her.

"God, I've missed you, Liv," Emily whispered in her ear before running her tongue around the rim, eliciting another involuntary moan from her. "You're off for the next week, right?"

"Yes." She rolled over and put her arms around Em, pulling her close. She kissed her neck, slowly moving her lips up to Em's ear. She wanted to be angry about the things Em had said to upset Kim, but at the moment, she was doing such wonderful things to her body Liv was having a hard time concentrating on anything else. "You feel so good."

"I have big plans for you, Agent Andrews." Em's hands moved down to Liv's bare ass. "This is going to be a birthday you'll remember for the rest of your life."

"My birthday isn't until Tuesday." Liv cocked her head to one side. "That's still five days away."

"You won't be getting out of bed until you need to go back to work on Wednesday," she promised with a slap on Liv's bare skin. "Take this shirt off now."

Liv gave in, allowing her to take control, but she was exhausted. She'd been asleep for less than an hour and felt even more tired now than she had when she'd fallen into bed. The last case had drained everything out of her, and she really didn't want to do anything but sleep. She'd been hoping all the way home that Em would stay at her own place and allow her time to regroup.

"Baby, I'm tired," she said when Em pushed her back down onto the bed after she'd removed her shirt. Her protest was half-hearted at best, because her body was responding in ways her brain didn't reciprocate when Em straddled her and began to rub her sex on Liv's abdomen.

"I have just what you need to remedy that." She kissed Liv's neck while she slid a hand between them and pushed inside Liv.

"Oh, fuck." Liv's hips thrust against Em's hand.

"Exactly." Em purred into Liv's ear. "I'm going to fuck you senseless. And then when you recover from that, I'm going to do it all over again. For the next. Five. Days."

"God, yes," Liv cried out, cursing her body for betraying her, but powerless to stop what Em had started.

All movement and feeling stopped when the shrill ring of her cell phone cut through the air. Two minutes earlier Liv would have welcomed the distraction, but now...*fuck.* She grabbed Emily's hand to stop its movement and rolled out from underneath her.

"Don't you dare answer that, Olivia."

"I have to, you know that. It's probably some loose ends on the case I just finished." Liv spared one last glance at the very fit body lying naked on her bed before answering the phone. She made her way to the bathroom and closed the door behind her. "Andrews."

"Liv, it's Davidson. We have a new case for you and your team."

"Jesus, Hal." Liv looked in the mirror. Her blond hair was getting a bit too long. It was down to her collar now, and she hated it that length. "Where's Blue Team? Isn't it their turn? I'm supposed to have the week off."

"I know, and I can't apologize enough. We believe this abduction is related to the Henderson case. You know we want to keep the same team on connected cases whenever possible. So yes, even though it should be Blue Team's case, we need you."

"What's the link?" She glanced at the door, hearing the unmistakable sounds of Emily putting her clothes back on. She could also hear the expletives Em wasn't attempting to keep quiet.

"A witness saw a man in his mid-thirties walking with a kid and a puppy in the vicinity of the abduction a few minutes before it was reported." Liv waited for him to go on. Papers rustled on the other end of the line, probably Hal trying to find something important on his cluttered desk, since he could usually remember minor details without his notes. "Unfortunately, no one got a plate number, or even a good look at the guy or the car, other than it was a green pickup. According to our witness, the kid was holding his hand as they walked down the street."

"Are we even sure the kid the witness saw was the kid that was taken?" Liv looked at her reflection in the mirror again. Her green eyes were dull, the spark of youth lost years ago. She'd seen too many things in this job to maintain any kind of innocence. "I mean, seriously, Hal. Kids do go for walks with their parents on occasion."

"Liv, that would fall under the category of coincidence, and I know how you feel about that word. Besides, this one is in the neighboring county from where the Henderson kidnapping was, and the witness's description of the kid matched the one the mother provided."

Liv closed her eyes and slowly shook her head. She seriously needed a break after the Henderson case. They'd found the little girl, but she'd been dead for three days. It was always rough when they recovered a body as opposed to rescuing a child. If they didn't find a body, the child might be alive somewhere.

"Give me the details," she finally said. This wouldn't go over well with Em, but she would never turn down a case. After feeling thrown away as a child, she'd joined the FBI and become a member of one of the bureau's CARD teams, or Child Abduction Rapid Deployment team, focused on returning children to the parents who loved them. She was honored to be part of one of only six CARD units in the country. "But Hal, I'm giving you ample notice. I'm taking some personal time after this one."

Liv emerged from the bathroom a few minutes later, meeting Em's hostile gaze unflinchingly. Without a word, she got dressed.

"Gee, let me guess," Em said. "You've been called away on a case. Don't they have anyone else who can do your job?"

"Em—"

"No, I don't want to hear it. We haven't spent more than a few hours together at a time in almost a year. You were supposed to be off for the next week."

"Emily, listen to me." Liv desperately wanted a drink, but that would be ill-advised with a new case on the line. Her head was beginning to pound, but she ignored the pain.

"No, *you* listen. I've continuously put my life on hold so I could be here for you whenever you needed me. When do you return the favor?"

"Soon, baby. This case is related to the last one. Someone took a kid from a park in Walton Creek. I need to go there tonight."

"Where the hell is Walton Creek?"

"About two hours from here, in Lehigh County, but that's not important. As soon as this case is over, I'm taking time off. I made sure Hal knows that."

"I may not be here when *this* case is over, Liv. I'm not sure I can do it anymore." Em looked like she was about to cry and Liv began to panic. She was so not good with the whole emotional thing. Nothing made her more uncomfortable than a crying woman.

"Please, you have to understand where I'm coming from. We're talking about my job. You knew that when we got together." Liv went to her and tried to embrace her, but she backed away, shaking her head.

"Do you know how many times you've thrown that in my face? Yes, I knew what your job was, but I didn't know it meant I would practically never see you because of it. I really can't deal with this anymore. I need someone who'll be here for me when I need her."

"So, what are you saying? You're breaking up with me?" It surprised Liv to realize her chest didn't ache at the thought.

"Yeah. If you leave tonight, I won't be here when you get back." Emily put one hand on her hip and raised an eyebrow.

Liv stared at her for a moment, wondering precisely what Em expected to happen. It wasn't like she could just walk away from her job—her *career,* for God's sake—and spend the rest of her days working in a coffee shop.

"I have to go," she said quietly. She hoped her eyes showed the proper amount of remorse, but she just wanted to pack her bag and get on the road. The sooner she got to Walton Creek, the sooner they could crack the case and get back home.

It used to scare her to realize she could shut down her emotions, but over the years she'd come to appreciate that ability. It helped her do her job. She honestly felt bad for the people whose kids were abducted, but if she let those things get to her, she wouldn't be as effective as she was. The downside was times like this when she should show emotion, but without even thinking, she shut down that part of her brain. It infuriated Emily but was the only way she could leave quickly. "You'll understand when you've had some time to think."

"I can't believe you just said that. Haven't the past two years meant anything to you?"

"I'm not doing this right now. I have to pack." Liv turned and began to toss clothes into a new duffel bag—the laundry from the one she'd just brought home would have to wait until later.

"I can't believe you're just going to walk out on me." Em stood next to the dresser, and Liv stopped to look at her, one hand resting on the handle to her underwear drawer.

"You're the one walking out on me." She kept her voice utterly calm. No emotion. "I'm just doing my job."

"Oh, that's classic. It's all my fault, right?" Em held Liv's gaze.

Emily was beautiful, she couldn't deny that. Liv had considered herself lucky when they'd first gotten together. Emily's auburn hair and green eyes had attracted her, and the fiery personality Em was displaying now had hooked her. Life was certainly never dull with Emily around. Standing there now, caught in a stare-down, Liv admitted to herself that Emily deserved better. Liv could never give her everything she deserved. She could never give her herself.

"Are you telling me your job is more important to you than I am?"

"That's not fair, Emily."

"Isn't it? If I were in the hospital with a life-threatening injury, would you forsake your damn job to be by my side?"

She wanted to say yes. It was the right answer, given the situation, but she couldn't. So far into the relationship, she should have answered easily, but the job came first, and it always would. Deep down she had always hoped she would find a woman who could become the most important thing in her life, but it would never happen. She resigned herself to that knowledge. She stayed silent and kept packing.

"Fuck you, Special Agent Olivia Andrews. I can't believe I've wasted this much time with you." Em turned on her heel and stormed out of the apartment.

Liv took a step toward the door, but quickly regained her senses. When Emily was pissed, it was best to leave her alone. Liv finished packing. No doubt she would be coming back to an empty apartment.

Liv had been honest with Emily from the beginning. They hadn't had a forever kind of relationship. It was fun, and mutually satisfying. She'd perfected the art of keeping the women in her life out of her heart. She'd spent too much time in her youth being abandoned, and she wasn't about to give a lover that kind of power.

CHAPTER FOUR

S ophie, baby, why do you torture yourself like this?"
"Because a part of me really wants to see if we can bridge
the gap between us." Sophie Kane fell back on the couch and put
her feet up on the coffee table. She was beat and wanted nothing
more than a few hours of down time to relax, but her older sister,
Barbara, had called almost the second she walked through the door
to her apartment.

She'd spent the past eight years working as a field agent for
the FBI in New York City. Sophie had only arrived back home to
Philadelphia a couple of weeks before, and she'd just started her
hostage-negotiator training two days ago. She was enjoying the
change of pace, but she was also looking forward to having the
weekend off.

"Jesus, you're still trying to gain their acceptance?" Barb
laughed in an obvious attempt to soften her words, and Sophie let
out an annoyed chuckle of her own, but the comment hurt. It hurt
more than Barbara, with her perfect life, could ever know. Barb
had a loving husband she'd been married to almost twenty-five
years, a son beginning his junior year of college at Penn State, and
a daughter set on graduating high school at the top of her class this
year. Barb had no idea how deeply being kicked out of the house
at age sixteen had wounded her. Barb had been twenty-four at the
time, with a baby on the way. She hadn't hesitated to take Sophie in,
and she would be forever grateful for her sister's generosity. But no,

Barb could never begin to comprehend the pain of being an absolute stranger to their own parents.

"They'll never come around, will they?" Sophie asked quietly, her eyes closed as she fought back the tears.

"Sweetie, Mom asked about you the other day, so you never know," Barb said, and Sophie could almost hear the shrug in her tone of voice. "Stranger things have happened."

"Not in my lifetime they haven't," she murmured, and picked up the beer she'd opened right before the phone rang. "Just out of curiosity, what did she ask?"

"How you were doing. If you were happy. If you'd found a man yet." Barb laughed as she said the last bit, and Sophie rolled her eyes.

"They'll never get it, will they?" She took a big drink from her beer and slammed the bottle down on the end table.

"Sweetie, don't beat yourself up over it, all right?" Barb sighed, her disappointment with their parents evident. "You're right, they'll never get it, and you'll just drive yourself crazy."

"Damn it, Barb, it's their forty-fifth wedding anniversary. They're my parents whether they want to admit it or not. How much of a scene would they cause in a public place if I just showed up unannounced?"

"They probably wouldn't because you know how important appearances are to them, and honestly, that might be the best plan, if you really have your heart set on showing up. If I ask them ahead of time, they'll say no. And they'd probably revoke my invitation too."

"Okay, then, it's settled." Sophie glanced at the photo of her parents she kept on the end table—a silent reminder of a past life. A life so long ago she'd almost forgotten the sound of her mother's voice. The picture of them at a Phillies game was the only shot of her parents she'd bothered to keep, and it had been taken only a couple of weeks before life as Sophie knew it came to a horrific end when she'd come out to them. "I'll meet you outside *Le Bec Fin* at seven o'clock on their anniversary."

"Fine. I know you well enough not to try to talk you out of it. I'll pretend I don't know anything and be as surprised as everyone else to see you there."

"Thanks. I can't explain why, but I'm at a point in my life where I can't move forward until I settle things with them once and for all." Sophie put the cold bottle against her forehead and closed her eyes. "I don't understand why they continue to shut me out of their lives. I haven't talked to them in over twenty years. How can anyone do that to their own child?"

"I don't have an answer. I couldn't do it to my kids, no matter what the circumstances."

Sophie turned her attention to the vibrating cell phone skittering across the coffee table.

"Damn it," she said in annoyance. "I have to go, Barb. My work cell is ringing. I'll call you in a few days."

She shut the cordless phone off and reached for the cell, knowing when she saw Hal Davidson's name displayed that she wouldn't get the relaxing weekend she'd hoped to have.

"Kane," she said.

"Sophie, it's Hal. How are things going with the training?"

"Fine, but I'm sure that isn't the reason you're calling, is it?" She walked to the kitchen, holding the beer bottle loosely in her hand.

"You know me too well," Hal said with a chuckle. "Your brother-in-law has told you too much about me, I see."

"You forget that I knew you before Jay ever told me anything about how you work." Sophie smiled wearily as she propped herself against the counter. "But you're right that he warned me before I came back here. Tell me what you need."

"For you to join a CARD team."

"But—"

"This might be a temporary assignment, so I've called in a couple of favors. We've put your hostage-negotiator training on hold until the case is closed. My team is down a person due to retirement, and we haven't brought anyone in to fill the spot yet. You might just be perfect for it, so I figured this case could be a trial for you and the team leader."

"No."

"Excuse me?"

"I want to be a negotiator, Hal. I moved back to Philly so I could do that. I don't want to be an agent working in the field every day anymore. I need some kind of stability in my life. I mean, Jesus, Hal, what if I don't want to be on a CARD team? Don't you think you're making a pretty huge career decision for me?"

She listened while he moved some papers around, shaking her head in defeat as she padded back to the living room to sink into her comfortable couch.

"You're absolutely right, Sophie," he said after a moment. "It won't be a permanent assignment. I'll keep looking for a replacement, and when the case is over, you can go right back to your training, if that's really what you want."

"You swear it's only for one case?" she asked, not quite believing him, but what choice did she have? He was her superior and ultimately she had to follow orders.

"I promise." He laughed quietly and was no doubt shaking his head. "Jay should have warned *me* about how *you* work."

"Why me? Don't you have someone else who might actually want to do this one?"

"You did a great job as an undercover agent in New York. You aren't afraid to speak your mind, and quite frankly, this team needs someone like you. A fresh set of eyes, so to speak. You can bring a new perspective to the case. I have a feeling we're dealing with a serial abductor, and honestly, my team may be too close to the situation."

"You said this would be a trial for me and the team leader. Is he a problem?" Sophie liked the sound of this assignment less and less as she learned more about the case.

"On the contrary, Olivia Andrews is probably my best agent." Hal sounded sincere but Sophie wasn't convinced. "They just finished a case which turned out badly, and one of her team members has retired. I need someone to fill in. She doesn't always deal very well with change, and having you on the team will definitely be a change."

"How so?"

"You're not only someone new, but you're also a woman. She's been dealing with a crew of men since she became team leader."

Sophie was pleased that the team leader was a woman, but she was less than enthusiastic after Hal's explanation. Apparently Agent Andrews disliked other women. Wonderful, she thought.

"Where do I need to go?" She closed her eyes and resigned herself to having to place her own goals on the back burner again. She'd been afraid it was too good to be true when negotiator training became available.

She was so tired of being an investigator in the field and was seriously looking forward to being a specialized agent, only called to a site when needed. She rarely spent more than a few days at a time in whatever place she called home and wanted a more stable life. At thirty-five, she still wanted to have a child but would never do that on her own. However, finding a woman to settle down and start a family with was proving harder than she'd anticipated. Not many women were willing to put up with an FBI field agent's tumultuous schedule.

"You're the best, Sophie. Drive to a little town in the Lehigh Valley called Walton Creek. It's not far from Allentown but is well off the beaten track, so it's actually a fairly isolated area. Like I said, the team leader is Olivia Andrews, and you'll check in with her when you get there."

Sophie found a pen and wrote down all the information he thought she needed before going to her bedroom and packing. With any luck, they wouldn't be away from home more than a couple of days, but she didn't hold out much hope after Hal filled her in on how the previous case had ended for Agent Andrews's team.

CHAPTER FIVE

L iv grabbed the hotel room key from the desk clerk, feeling as though she hadn't slept in days. Before she slid the key completely into the lock, the door opened, causing her to jump back in surprise.

"Jesus," she muttered, a hand on her throat. The first thing she noticed was that the woman standing on the other side of the door was gorgeous, with brown hair and eyes the color of dark chocolate. The small grin indicated her amusement at Liv's surprised reaction. That grin pissed Liv off. She definitely wasn't in the mood for surprises. She held the key up with the tag clearly stating the room number and tapped the number on the door with her knuckle before meeting the woman's gaze once again. "You're in my room."

"No," the woman said with a quick shake of her head. "I'm in *our* room. I presume you're Olivia Andrews?"

"Apparently I'm at a disadvantage. You are?"

"Special Agent Sophie Kane." She held out a hand, and Liv grasped it firmly. "It's a pleasure to meet you."

"Likewise." She was definitely going to have to speak with Hal about sticking someone on her team without her input. Yes, they needed another member since Randy had retired, but it was totally unacceptable for Hal to spring someone on her like this. She should have a say in who would work for her. She walked past Sophie into the room and dropped her duffel on the empty bed. "I thought I'd sit in on interviews for Randy's replacement. I didn't know Hal had found anyone yet."

"He hasn't." Sophie took a seat on her own bed. "For some reason he seems to think I may be a good fit for your team, so he's apparently decided to throw me into the thick of things. My brother-in-law is a friend of Hal's. I'm supposed to be training as a hostage negotiator, but that's been put on hold until this case is closed."

Liv stared at her in silence, wondering why she thought Liv would care about the inner workings of her family and their friendships. She sat down and leaned forward, holding her head in her hands.

"And why exactly does Hal think you're the right one for this case?"

"He thinks I'm a good investigator and that I can bring a new perspective."

"A new perspective." Liv laughed without humor but didn't look up. "And fresh eyes? Did he lay that line on you too?"

"Yes, he did," Sophie said. She hesitated before continuing. "I don't understand."

Liv raised her head to look at Sophie. She smiled wryly and shook her head before placing a hand on the back of her neck and trying to knead the tight muscles there.

"He tells the same thing to everyone he places on one of these teams. Don't go thinking you're special just because he gave you that line of crap." She took a deep breath and looked over at the clock on the nightstand between the beds. They needed to get to the police station soon. "Have you ever worked a child-abduction case before?"

"No," Sophie answered, her tone clipped.

"Fuck me," Liv said under her breath. It wasn't enough for Hal to have assigned a new agent to her team without her input, but he'd assigned one with no experience in what they were doing. She lowered her head into her hands again.

"Are you okay?"

"Headache." Liv answered without looking up. "And I'm tired. We just finished a case and—"

"Kendra Henderson, I know. It's never easy when a victim turns up dead, but it's even worse when it's a young child." Sophie shrank back visibly when Liv leveled a stare at her.

"You won't last long on my team if you make a habit of interrupting me."

"Maybe I didn't make myself clear," Sophie said, sitting up a bit straighter and not bothering to hide her annoyance—a fact that irritated Liv. In fact, it seemed like everything about Sophie Kane bothered her. "This is a temporary assignment. I'm not going to change who I am just to keep you happy, Agent Andrews. If things aren't working out, then I just won't be assigned to your team any longer."

"I wouldn't count on that, but nevertheless, I don't like being interrupted when I'm speaking."

"Understood."

Agent Kane was cute when she was annoyed—just one more thing that irritated Liv. Apparently it would be difficult to not like her. Maybe that's exactly what Hal had in mind.

"Do I need to know anything else in order to stay on your good side, Agent Andrews?"

"Two things, actually. Since we're obviously going to be roommates for the foreseeable future, call me Liv."

"Okay. And the second?"

"If you snore, I'm throwing you out on your ass and you can sleep in your car." Liv headed to the bathroom, but her step faltered when she heard Agent Kane's mumbled response.

"I hope to God you don't talk in your sleep since I can't interrupt you."

Liv swallowed her chuckle as she shut the door behind her.

CHAPTER SIX

M ark jumped when the phone rang. He hadn't meant to
fall asleep. He checked the door to the basement to make
sure it was locked before he picked up the phone.

"Yeah," he said.

"I tried to call you earlier this afternoon," a deep voice said
from the other end of the line. "The deal fell through and we don't
need the little boy."

"What?" Mark's hands began to shake. "I already got him."

Silence. A bit of a commotion sounded in the background,
but Mark couldn't make out what anyone was saying. He wiped a
sweaty palm on his pant leg.

"What am I supposed to do with the kid?"

"I know you already got him, you fucking idiot. It's all over the
news. You've practically led them to your goddamned front door.
But you know what? It's not my problem what you do with him, is
it, Mark? Kill him. Or keep him. We might be able to use him soon.
It's all the same to me, but just remember those are your only two
choices. You let him go, and he leads the FBI right to you and you
lead them to me in return. That is not acceptable, Mark. I moved you
into that secluded house with the nice big basement. You can lock
him down there until he rots, and no one will ever know he's there.
But you let him go, and you and your mother both die. Don't think
for a second that I *need* you for any of this, Marcus. I have others
working for me too, and I can replace you in a heartbeat."

Mark held the phone to his ear for a few moments after the other man hung up. He really didn't want to have to kill another kid. Maybe he *could* keep him locked up in the basement for a while. He could save him for the next call that came in.

❖

"Hey, Boss," Justin said when Liv walked into the police station with Sophie right behind her. He moved in close so only Liv could hear him. "Who's the newbie?"

"Randy's replacement. A friend of a friend of Hal's, or something." She gave an indifferent shrug.

"Excuse me," Sophie said, placing a hand on Liv's shoulder. Justin turned his head to hide a grin when Liv rolled her eyes in annoyance before turning to look at her. "I'm not *a friend of a friend* of anyone. I'm a member of this team, hopefully temporarily, and would appreciate being treated as such."

"Then you can make your own introductions, because I have a case to work." Liv gestured to Justin. "This is my second in command, Justin Ingram. Justin, Sophie Kane. You're on your own with the rest of the team."

Liv saw Gabe Lloyd wave at her from an open doorway and went to greet him.

"Are we all set up?" she asked.

"No, Sergeant Dickhead has been on the phone for the past twenty minutes, and they won't let us set up our equipment until he gives the okay."

"Oh, God, please tell me that's not really his name," Liv said, glancing over her shoulder at the office Gabe indicated.

"No, just an analysis of his less-than-stellar personality."

"Don't tease me like that." Liv took a deep breath and headed for the closed door.

"Ma'am, you can't go in there," a female officer said just before she grasped the knob. Liv hesitated when she saw the obvious panic written all over the young woman's face. "Please."

Liv reached into her pocket and pulled out her badge, but the woman didn't seem fazed and continued to explain why Liv couldn't go inside. She stepped away from the door just as it opened, and a rather rotund man wearing a nametag declaring him Sgt. Mansfield walked out. The man's grimace indicated he despised working with the FBI, but that was hardly anything new. Most cops did. He walked right past Liv without so much as a glance and headed right for Gabe.

"Agent Lloyd, I'm so sorry to keep you and your team waiting. I'm Sergeant Robert Mansfield," he said as he grasped Gabe's hand and shook it vigorously. He turned and walked toward an open door in the back of the station, motioning for Gabe to follow him. "You can bring your people into the conference room and we'll get started."

Gabe looked to Liv for guidance, but she merely shook her head slightly, indicating that he should take the lead. It wasn't the first time someone had wrongfully assumed Gabe, now the oldest agent of the group since Randy retired, was the team leader. Liv decided to see just how deep a hole Sergeant Mansfield could dig for himself. Gabe smiled knowingly before he gathered everyone to follow him into the conference room. Liv ignored the quizzical look on Sophie's face and walked into the room.

Conference room was a generous way to describe the area Liv found herself in. A single table had eight chairs squeezed in around it, and a dirty coffee pot in the corner of the room looked like it had about three years' worth of mold growing in it. The sink next to it didn't look much better. A dry-erase board hung between two windows and looked like the officers wrote their lunch orders on it. Liv took a seat at the heavily scarred table and waited. Gabe sat directly across from her, and Sophie took the chair to her right.

The other men remained standing as the young officer who had stopped Liv from entering Mansfield's office came in and took the seat to Liv's left.

"This is Officer Beth Parsons," Mansfield said, without looking at her, when everyone was finally seated. "She'll be your liaison with the department. I hope that's not a problem?"

"Not at all," Gabe said.

Mansfield got right down to business. "The boy's name is Timothy York."

Liv didn't care much for the sergeant. Not just that he didn't feel the need to introduce himself to everyone, but he looked a little too smug and hadn't yet met her eyes as he spoke. Not just her eyes, but Sophie's and Officer Parsons's as well. His beer gut made it difficult for him to reach the table properly. He was probably close to retirement age, a guess based on his silver hair—what little there was of it—and the wrinkles around his eyes. She decided the charade had gone on long enough, and it was time to let him know who was running the investigation, because she certainly didn't want him to think it was him.

"He was taken from Walton Park earlier this afternoon," Mansfield said.

"What time did the abduction happen?" Liv sat back in her chair, her fingers interlaced on the table in front of her. Mansfield kept his eyes on Gabe for a moment, no doubt waiting for him to remind her who was in charge. She waited with growing impatience until Mansfield finally looked at her.

"I'm sorry—who are you, honey?" he asked, his eyes fixated on her chest before moving back up to her face. Liv barely managed to tamp down her disgust.

"Special Agent Olivia Andrews, Sergeant Mansfield. I'm the team leader here, and I would appreciate it if you would direct your briefing to me from here on out. And I'm not your honey."

"What is this, some kind of joke?" He laughed, but his joviality quickly died down when he saw no one was laughing with him. He looked at Gabe. "You work *under* her?"

Gabe squirmed a bit in his seat and simply nodded once. Liv gave him credit for keeping his cool. The last time someone questioned the hierarchy in their group, Gabe had him against the wall with a forearm pressed to his throat for the derogatory name directed at Liv. The team had come together like a family, and they all looked out for one another. It was obvious Gabe wanted desperately to say something to Mansfield, but Liv shook her head almost imperceptibly.

"Un-fucking-believable," Mansfield muttered under his breath. He shook his head and looked down at his notes.

"Do we have a problem here, Sergeant?" Liv glared at him and he backed down immediately.

"No, ma'am," he said with another glance at her chest.

"I'd appreciate it if you'd look me in the eye when you address me, Sergeant," she said, ignoring Sophie's chuckle. "Unless I'm mistaken, my tits have nothing to do with the reason we're here. So I'll ask you again—do we have a problem here, Sergeant?"

"No, ma'am, we don't," he said, his face turning red as he met her eyes.

"Good, then I'll repeat my other question—what time did the abduction occur?" Liv sighed audibly when he began to shuffle through the papers in front of him. "Sergeant Mansfield, do you have so many kidnappings in your little town that you can't remember what time of day this one happened?"

Officer Parsons came to the rescue, stopping Mansfield from the tirade he'd obviously been about to begin if his sputtering was any indication. "The mother, Abby York, says they arrived at the park around two thirty this afternoon." Liv turned in her seat to better see the woman sitting next to her. "According to her, Timmy was playing on the jungle gym while she was visiting with a friend. She doesn't remember seeing him after three o'clock, but the abduction wasn't called in until around three thirty."

"Is the park fenced?" Liv asked, knowing it was too much to ask for.

"No, ma'am. It's surrounded by trees and other foliage."

"Gabe, I want you and Ingram out there, now." Liv paused while the two men exited the room. They already knew what she needed them to do. She looked at her watch. Already after nine. The first twelve hours were critical in cases like this, and they had already lost the first six. She hoped Mansfield's people hadn't trampled all over the scene.

She turned her attention to the sergeant, but made sure to glance at Parsons periodically so she wouldn't feel ignored. It would also send a message to Mansfield that she wasn't about to let him dictate the rules.

"I was told someone saw a man walking to a pickup truck with a young boy and a puppy near the scene. The boy fit the description of Timmy York. Does anyone have a description of the man, or even the pickup he was driving?"

Both officers shook their heads.

Liv closed her eyes and rubbed her temples, trying her best to stave off the headache she'd felt coming on before she'd even left Philadelphia. "We'll need this room for our command center. Please just leave your files here, and we'll go over them."

"Do you have any idea how long you'll be here?" Mansfield asked before exiting the room.

Liv let loose a short bark of laughter before she stood to face him. It gave her some sense of satisfaction that at five-foot-eleven she was a good three inches taller than he was.

"We have a missing child, Sergeant. Are you looking for a psychic prediction, or do you honestly think I can tell you we'll be out of your hair in the next day or two?"

"What hair?" Sophie muttered quietly enough that he couldn't hear her. Liv caught it though and fought the smile that tugged at the corners of her mouth. Maybe Sophie would fit in after all.

He mumbled something resembling an apology as he walked out the door, leaving it open in his wake. Liv went to shut it, motioning at the same time for Officer Parsons to be seated again.

"Did you need something from me, ma'am?" she asked, looking nervously from one agent to the next, her gaze finally settling on Sophie. Parsons was attractive, but Liv didn't like the way she kept staring at Sophie. Sophie was busy perusing one of the files and didn't seem to notice the attention, but Liv did.

"Is there somewhere around here we can get some decent coffee, and maybe some sandwiches or something?" Liv asked. She stood at the head of the table, resting her hands flat on the surface in front of her. "I have a feeling we're going to be here for a while."

They wrote down what they wanted, ordering extra for Gabe and Justin, and she sent her other team member, Victor Nathan, to get the food. Frank Franklin, the team's tech guru, finished setting up the electronic equipment in their new command center. It irked

Liv that they could have had most of it set up and running already if Mansfield hadn't been intent on his power trip.

"Officer Parsons, I want to thank you for the information you gave us." Liv took a seat before pulling a bottle of aspirin from her pocket and dry-swallowing two of the pills. "I know not many local LEOs want to deal with us, so how did you end up with the short stick?"

"Ma'am?"

"You keep calling me that, and I'll refuse to answer. It's Andrews, all right?" At the young woman's nod, Liv continued. "Why did Mansfield stick you with us? What did you do to piss him off?"

"I think my being a woman pisses him off," Parsons said. As soon as the words were out there, she sat up straight and looked mortified.

Liv chuckled. "Relax, Parsons, he's not the first man I've run across who thinks a woman's place is *anywhere* but law enforcement, trust me." Liv glanced over at Sophie, who was still busy going through the file they had on the York case. "This is Agent Sophie Kane."

Sophie raised her head and smiled. "Call me Kane." Liv didn't miss the look shared between the two of them. If that look meant what she thought it did, she'd have to nip it in the bud. She made herself a mental note to speak to Sophie about it later. It was one thing for Parsons to show an interest, but if one of her agents returned that interest, there would be a problem. Not only did it present an ethical problem, but it would also be a distraction. "Is there anything you can think of that hasn't made it into the file yet?"

"No." Parsons shook her head. "The parents' address and home phone number are there. Sergeant Mansfield has spoken with them already, but I assume you'll want to interview them too?"

"Yes, tonight, if at all possible. Can you call them and let them know we'll be dropping by?" Liv reached for the papers Sophie had already set aside. An Amber alert had been issued soon after the boy had been reported missing, but there hadn't been any tangible leads so far, save the one from the witness who saw them walking from the park. It was going to be a hell of a long night.

CHAPTER SEVEN

It was close to ten when Liv sat next to Sophie on a couch in the Yorks' living room. She took the offered coffee because Abby York had probably made it especially for them after she got the call from Officer Parsons. Liv hoped to hell she was drinking decaf, because she fully intended to get at least a couple of hours' sleep before the sun came up.

"Is there any news?" Abby asked, looking close to hysteria. Liv noted the red-rimmed eyes—obvious evidence she had been crying pretty much nonstop since her boy went missing.

"I'm sorry, Mrs. York, but there's nothing yet." Liv placed her coffee cup atop a coaster on the table before pulling a notepad out of her inside breast pocket. "We need to get some information from you."

"We already spoke with Sergeant Mansfield for over two hours," Peter York said, his tone brusque and waving his hand abruptly.

Did he know his wife's nerves were frayed, or did he have something to hide?

"I understand that you're upset, Mr. York," Liv said.

"I'm just not sure what else we can tell you." His voice caught.

"I know this is a difficult time for you, but we're doing everything we can to find your son. You may have some small piece of information you didn't think was pertinent at the time of your interview with Sergeant Mansfield that could help us." Sophie smiled warmly at them. "Please just bear with us, and we'll be out of here as soon as we can."

Liv spared a glance at Sophie. If left to her own devices, she might say the wrong thing and end up sounding insensitive. She definitely lacked people skills, but apparently Sophie Kane had them in spades.

"Is Timmy your biological child?" Liv asked, quickly turning her attention back to the parents.

"He's mine, not Peter's," Abby replied.

Liv exchanged a quick glance with Sophie before writing down that bit of news. They were only two minutes into their interview and already had a piece of information Mansfield hadn't included with the initial police reports.

"What the hell does that have to do with anything?" Peter asked, looking back and forth between them. "I may not be his biological father, but I'm the only father he's ever known. I love him like he was my own."

"I understand, Mr. York, but we need to know—is his biological father in his life at all?" Sophie asked. Abby shook her head in response. "Is it at all possible he could have taken Timmy?"

"That son of a bitch never wanted anything to do with his son," Peter said, his face turning red. "He didn't even believe Timmy was his. He accused Abby of cheating on him."

"Even so, if you have an address or a phone number for him, we're going to need it." Sophie was still writing, but she glanced up as she spoke.

"I have no idea where he is." Abby looked at her husband, who appeared more perturbed with every passing second. "I can get you his lawyer's name and number though."

"That would be great," Liv said.

Peter fumed. "This is ridiculous."

Liv couldn't blame him for being angry. She couldn't begin to imagine how it must feel to go through this.

"Please, you have to find Timmy." Abby reached for a tissue and dabbed gingerly at the tears in her eyes. The action was obviously a habit, because if she was trying not to smudge her makeup, it was far too late for that. "He needs his medication."

"Medication? Timmy's ill?" Liv frowned. Something else not included in the reports. *Christ, it's more like the Henderson case than we realized.*

"He has some mild mental disabilities which aren't obvious when you first meet him. He also has anger issues, which is what the medication is for." Abby finally abandoned the tissue and wiped her tears on the sleeve of her sweatshirt. "Please. You have to find him."

Liv looked at Sophie, who was probably thinking the same thing if she was as caught up on the case as Liv hoped she was. Kendra Henderson had suffered from autism. A child abducted in Monroe County about a month earlier had turned up dead as well. That one suffered from Asperger's syndrome, but they'd never found anything else to connect the two cases. Whoever was taking these kids apparently didn't want the ones with health issues, whether mental or physical. Kendra had probably been killed because of her disability. If the kids' disabilities had been obvious, then she might think they were being abducted *because* they were damaged in some way. But that didn't seem to be the case. Hopefully Frank was piecing together some kind of pattern. She'd welcome any kind of lead to follow up on.

"What about the phone lines?" Peter asked after a moment.

"Excuse me?" Liv turned her attention back to him.

"Sergeant Mansfield said the FBI would probably use some tracing equipment on our phones. In case we get a ransom demand."

"Have there been any calls?" Liv didn't try to hide her skepticism. Kidnapping for ransom usually happened only in wealthy families and in other countries where a victim was held for obscene amounts of money or weapons by armed guerillas, usually working for drug lords.

"No," Abby said softly.

"With all due respect, if this was about money, you would have already received—"

Liv looked at Sophie's hand on her forearm.

"Would you excuse us a moment?" Sophie smiled apologetically at the Yorks before standing and tilting her head toward the front door. Liv was angry at the interruption but forced herself to smile at them before she followed. Outside, with the door closed behind them, she dropped the façade.

"What the hell are you doing?"

"Their son has been abducted," Sophie said, her voice barely above a whisper but her irritation with Liv's insensitivity obvious. "If having tracers on their phones makes them feel better, then why not just do it?"

"Because it's a waste of time and money—you know that as well as I do. How many kids are abducted in this country for ransom? If they wanted money, they would have gone after someone high profile, not some small-town diner owner and doctor's office receptionist." Liv worked hard at keeping her voice low so the Yorks wouldn't overhear but was having a hard time pushing her frustration aside. She paced in front of Sophie, who leaned against the porch railing, looking sexy as hell. Liv shook her head to clear it. She sure as shit didn't need a distraction like that now. "And I don't want to have to tell you for a third time to never interrupt me again. Especially when I'm talking to a victim's family."

"I'm sorry. You're right, and it won't happen again. I just don't see the harm in giving them peace of mind. To them it looks as though we aren't doing anything other than interviewing them over and over. If it makes them feel better to have their phone lines bugged, why not?"

Liv bit her tongue when what she wanted more than anything to do was let loose with a string of obscenities. How dare Sophie try to undercut her authority? Liv looked at her truck parked in the driveway and took a deep breath in an attempt to calm herself and to slip her defenses into place. Emotion was incredibly draining.

"Fine," she said when she turned her attention back to Sophie. She forced a smile, but could tell by Sophie's expression it didn't reassure her. "I'll give in, Agent Kane, because I know how to pick my battles. I suggest you do the same, because this isn't worth fighting about."

Liv pulled out her cell and called Victor Nathan to come out and equip the phones. She stormed back into the house, not bothering to see if Sophie was following her. Once Victor arrived and got to work, she and Sophie continued to speak with the Yorks but were unable to get any other new information. Liv thanked them for their cooperation, and they left with a promise to notify them if they uncovered anything.

"Tell me your thoughts," Liv said when they were finally on the road heading back to the police station.

"I want off this team. It's obvious you and I will never see eye to eye on anything." Sophie spared a glance at Liv before redirecting her gaze to the road straight ahead of them.

"About the case, Kane." Liv gripped the steering wheel tight and took a deep breath. "We can deal with the other shit later."

"My gut tells me Kendra Henderson was probably killed because of her disability, and I doubt Timmy York's biological father had anything to do with his disappearance." Sophie glanced at her, but Liv kept her eyes glued to the road and nodded her agreement.

"A child in Monroe county a few weeks ago turned up dead too. We didn't work that case and got the Henderson one only because nothing linked the two. That boy in Monroe County had Asperger's."

"Jesus, Liv," Sophie whispered, all thoughts of leaving the team apparently gone, "when he finds out Timmy has a disability he's going to kill him."

"Then it's our job to find him before that happens."

❖

"Hey, Boss," Frank said when Liv and Sophie walked into their headquarters a few minutes later. "I might have discovered a pattern."

"Are Lloyd and Ingram back yet?" Liv took a seat and rubbed the back of her neck.

"We found some fishing line in an alley that looks like the kind we found at the Henderson scene, and a glove nearby too. I sent the glove to Allentown to be tested, but I doubt we'll get a hit. It looked like a glove a landscaper might wear, so it may not even belong to the kidnapper," Justin said as he came into the room and sat across from Liv. His close-cropped hair and the Semper Fi tattoo low on the right side of his neck made his Marine background obvious. He was thirty-two, and Liv loved him like a little brother.

"Did Mansfield's people even look for evidence at the scene?" Liv asked, slamming an open palm on the table. If the guy did leave a glove behind, maybe they'd get lucky with DNA inside it. "What's the pattern, Frank?"

"I've compiled a list of abductions within a hundred-mile radius of where we are now," he said, staring at his computer screen as he spoke. "There seems to be approximately two months between incidents—unless the child ends up dead, then the pattern usually accelerates. They only go back about a year, as near as I can tell. When one is found dead, another one is abducted within a week, give or take a day. Of course, that's assuming they're all related. Obviously our team hasn't worked every one of those cases, but I'm looking at a total of nine in the past twelve months, including the York kid. Three have turned up dead."

"We know about the Asperger's case and the Henderson girl's autism. Anything wrong with the third one that was killed?" Liv asked.

"He was deaf and mute." Frank sounded disgusted. "No sign of sexual abuse either, just like the other two."

"So if we recover Timmy York's body instead of rescuing him, we can expect another abduction about a week later, in the radius you mentioned." She sighed and rubbed her eyes. It seemed like she hadn't slept in days—and probably wouldn't get much sleep anytime soon. She stifled a yawn.

"What about the other five kids?" Sophie asked. "The ones who weren't found dead?"

"They haven't been found at all," Frank said quietly.

"So we're probably looking for someone who lives in the middle of where these are taking place." Liv spoke more to herself than to the others in the room. "We're close to the New Jersey border too. How many of them happened in Jersey?"

"Two there, and one in New York's southern tier," Frank said, still typing without looking up. "I'm not picking up anything south of Philadelphia or west of Harrisburg though."

"Which means we're pretty much in the middle of it right here. Any tangible leads on the cases we didn't work?" Liv moved to stand behind Frank and watch the computer screen over his shoulder.

"I haven't had a chance to check, but I will." He entered something more into his laptop.

Liv grimaced when she looked at the map someone had put up on the wall and saw the list of known pedophiles from the surrounding counties tacked up next to it. If this case was related to the previous two kidnappings, it wasn't a case of pedophilia, but they had to cover all their bases. They were more likely dealing with one of many cases of selling kids on the black market. Whether to the sick fucks who got their jollies by sexually abusing kids, human trafficking, or child slavery, she couldn't say for sure.

But she was fairly certain the person actually abducting these kids was *not* a pedophile, at least not the kind who got off on physical abuse. He could be the kind of sicko who made kid-on-kid porn to sell to other people, but the ones found dead so far hadn't shown any evidence of someone touching them sexually. And from the descriptions attached to each name on the map, their perp in this case was different. He clearly didn't get off on raping and beating young victims. "Gabe and Victor are interviewing the people on that list now." Frank removed his glasses and tossed them on the table in front of him. "Victor went to meet him as soon as he was finished at the York's place."

"Timmy York has mental disabilities," Liv said. "He also has anger issues and is on medication to control it. Apparently the disability isn't noticeable, but whoever took him is going to figure it out sooner or later, and we need to find him before then. If we don't, we'll probably have another dead child on our hands."

"Shit," Justin said, slamming a file on the table. "We're wasting time looking for pedophiles. Our perp either knows what he's doing or he's one lucky bastard. He disappears right from under us."

"Boss, you should go back to the motel and get a couple hours of sleep. We can handle things here." Frank put his glasses back on and returned his attention to the computer. Liv would have argued, but she was running on fumes—then again, they all were. The

Henderson case had just ended, and she hadn't been sleeping well. She doubted her team had either.

"Do I look that bad, Frank?" She grinned when he shrugged and didn't glance up at her. "Wake me up if anything breaks."

"You got it," Frank said, hiding his own grin.

"Oh, and before I forget, Peter York is not Timmy's bio dad." Liv pulled out the slip of paper Abby had written names and numbers on and handed it to Frank. "Here's his name, and his lawyer's name and number. Call the lawyer to find out where the dad is. We need to rule him out as a suspect."

"I'll get right on it."

"It's almost midnight," Sophie said.

"And your point is?" Liv asked rhetorically, facing her. Sophie shrank back a little, so Liv knew she understood. "We have a missing child, Kane. If we have to wake a few people up in the middle of the night in order to find him, then we will."

"Sorry," Sophie mumbled.

Liv knew she was only snapping at Sophie because she was tired. She looked around the room and saw Frank with his head buried in his computer and Justin suddenly finding something interesting in a file he was holding. After a deep calming breath, she softened her tone.

"We sleep in shifts, Sophie," she said as she pulled her keys from her pocket. She removed the key for her SUV and handed it to Sophie. "Since we drove here from the motel together, you can take my truck back later. I'll go with Justin now."

"Sure thing," Sophie said without meeting her eyes.

Liv stared at her for a moment, wondering where the Sophie Kane she'd met earlier in the evening had gone. That Sophie wouldn't be sitting there quietly without making her opinions known, the remark about it being the middle of the night aside. Liv looked at Justin, tilted her chin toward the door, and he followed her out without a word. She'd try to figure Sophie out later. Normally she and her second-in-command wouldn't take a sleeping shift together, but Gabe and Frank had enough experience to deal with anything that might come up. Besides that, she wanted to talk to Justin. They walked to his car, and he handed her his keys.

"How's Bill doing?" she asked when they got in.

"He's definitely not happy about all the time I've been away from home lately." Justin let his head rest on the back of the seat. "But he understands. How's Emily?"

Liv had never kept the fact that she was a lesbian from any of her team members. She didn't want any problems stemming from it and felt it was better to be open from the outset. Justin had been with her team longer than anybody, and they had always been able to talk about things that sometimes made the others uncomfortable. Like their respective partners.

"Not happy, and definitely not understanding." She pulled out of the parking lot and headed toward the motel. "Looks like I'm single yet again."

"That sucks," Justin said, looking at her. "Someday you'll find a woman who can understand. She's out there, Liv, you've just got to keep looking."

"Right."

"What about Sophie?"

She arched an eyebrow and glanced at him. "Other than the fact I know nothing about her, including whether or not she's even family, you know I refuse to get involved with anyone I work with. Especially not someone under my command."

"She's a looker though, isn't she?" he asked. She knew without looking at him that he was smiling. "You don't have to answer that, Boss. I'm just messing with you."

She sighed as Sophie's face flashed through her mind. She was definitely a looker. Maybe she didn't know for sure if Sophie was gay, but the look that passed between her and Officer Parsons had been pretty telling. Apparently Sophie wasn't interested in Liv though, and it wouldn't matter if she was. Sophie didn't even want to work with her, and the bureau frowned upon getting involved with other agents. Liv had experienced firsthand how it wasn't a good idea to mix business with pleasure. She smiled as she silently acknowledged being with Sophie Kane would probably be very pleasurable indeed but shook the thought from her head.

"What do you think he's doing with the kids?" Liv tried to focus her energies in the right direction.

"I wish I knew." Justin sounded as tired as she felt. "Any thoughts?"

"Too many possibilities to even consider, each one more terrifying than the last. I can't figure out why he's killing the kids with disabilities though. What if we're dealing with organ trafficking?" Liv tried to suppress a shudder but wasn't successful. "I was reading a magazine article about that going on in other countries. It's some scary shit."

"It might explain not wanting the damaged ones." Justin sat up a little straighter in his seat. "Thinking that one abnormality makes the whole undesirable. And there's always the pedophile angle," he said. "I mean, I know we're not dealing *directly* with a child rapist, but that doesn't mean he isn't taking them to provide some asshole with his playthings."

"Scary shit no matter what his reasons are," Liv said as she pulled into the motel parking lot. "I just hope we catch him before any more kids turn up dead."

CHAPTER EIGHT

L iv had left only thirty minutes earlier, and Sophie fought to keep her eyes open as she continued to look through everything they had on Timmy York's abduction. They had to be missing something. She glanced at the statistics Victor printed out for her, which were more than a little disheartening. Somewhere in the neighborhood of eight hundred thousand kids were reported missing or abducted every year in the United States alone. But it disturbed her most that in stereotypical kidnappings involving children, forty percent ended up dead. And of those, seventy-four percent were killed within the first three hours.

She pushed the thoughts away because she couldn't let those numbers mess with her head. She had to believe they'd find Timmy alive. She tried to wake herself up by taking a healthy swig from the cup of coffee next to her hand but grimaced and barely kept from gagging when the cold dregs slid down her throat.

"Why don't you go on back to the motel?" Gabe suggested as he tried to hide his chuckle with a cough. He'd returned to the station a few minutes after Liv and Justin left for the night. "I'm pretty sure nothing else is going to come up tonight. Frank, Victor, and I can handle things until morning."

"I'm okay." Sophie gave him a glare she hoped conveyed her annoyance and stretched her sore back muscles.

"Sure you are," Frank said, without looking away from his computer screen. "I can hear your eyelids sliding closed from over here. Sounds like sandpaper to me."

"You guys are probably more tired than I am."

"We're used to working all night," Gabe said.

"Leave her alone, Gabe. She's probably afraid of sharing a room with Liv." Frank peered over the top of the screen and grinned at her.

"I know I would be." Gabe nodded without looking up.

She looked from Frank to Gabe, wondering what there was to be afraid of. Liv was definitely an intense—and at times infuriating— person, but the time they shared in the car coming back from the Yorks' earlier had been mostly uneventful. She'd even decided, for the time being at least, not to call Hal about being removed from the team. Trying to tell herself it was simply because she felt bad for the Yorks would be a lie. Wanting to catch the guy who was cold enough to kill innocent children was definitely a factor. But the instant attraction she felt to Liv was playing a role in her decision too.

"He's just seeing how far he can push you, Kane. Ignore him." Gabe picked up the phone to answer a call with another tip from the Amber alert.

"Liv is harmless," Frank said. He shrugged before returning his attention to the computer screen. "Well, unless you snore, that is. Then you might very well find yourself waking up in the middle of the parking lot."

"Why am I sharing a room with her in the first place?" she asked, trying not to show her concern about his statement, especially after Liv's earlier warning about snoring. No one had ever told her she snored, but that didn't mean she didn't. "Shouldn't the team leader have her own room?"

"We all share rooms. It was Liv's idea, but she hasn't actually had to since we've only had men on the team," Frank said. "She says it creates a more family-like atmosphere. That and the fact that half the team is usually working all the time, there's no need for everyone to have their own place. I didn't like the idea at first, but it's grown on me. We're a close-knit team, and sharing rooms while we're on a case helps to keep it that way. As far as her having her own—why? She's hardly ever there. I swear she doesn't sleep more than a couple hours a night."

"Are you sure you don't mind if I go?" she asked. "I don't want to get anybody in trouble."

"Go. Victor's on his way back with more coffee and donuts, and don't you dare say how clichéd that is," Frank said. "Besides, until we get a credible lead we usually work three at a time for twelve-hour shifts."

She grabbed her coat from the back of her chair and jerked it on, worried they might change their minds and make her stay. Suddenly she couldn't resist the option of falling into bed. She waited long enough for Gabe to indicate the call was nothing before she made her way out to the parking lot and Liv's SUV. It was after midnight, and she really hoped Liv was asleep when she got there.

❖

When Sophie walked into the room, Liv was sitting at the small desk talking on her cell phone. She took the phone from her ear and looked at her quizzically.

"What are you doing here? Did something break on the case?"

"Frank and Gabe told me to take off for the night," she said. "Go back to your call."

Liv turned her back again and lowered her voice as Sophie gathered her things and went into the bathroom to change. She opened the door a crack when she heard Liv raise her voice, but stayed inside the bathroom where Liv couldn't see she was eavesdropping.

"Damn it, Mary, you know I can't help it. I would never disappoint her on purpose," Liv was saying. Sophie adjusted the door so she could see the reflection of Liv's back in the mirror. "A five-year-old kid was kidnapped today. It's not like I can just beg off work because I promised to take Kim to the ball game. My job doesn't work that way, and you know it."

Sophie wondered who she was talking to. Could it be a girlfriend? She shook her head. What did it matter? Liv was her superior as long as she was on her team, and anything personal between them would never fly. She couldn't deny that her stomach fluttered a bit whenever Liv looked at her though.

"Put her on the phone…I know what damn time it is, Mary, just put her on the phone," she said. Sophie saw her glance toward the bathroom before standing and walking out of her line of sight. She felt like an idiot trying to listen in, but she couldn't help herself.

"Kim, it's Liv. I'm really sorry, but I won't be able to go to the game tomorrow…I know I promised, but I…Kim, please listen to me…I promise I'll make it up to you."

Sophie was about to close the door again when she heard Liv sigh loudly. She risked a look and saw Liv sitting on the edge of her bed, her back to her.

"Kim, I'm sorry. I don't know what else to say. There's been another kidnapping and I have to work. I'll be home as soon as I possibly can, and we'll go to a game, all right? God, please don't cry, Kim."

It was ridiculous to be hiding in the bathroom, so she quickly changed into her usual sweat pants and a T-shirt before walking back out into the room and getting into her bed. She curled up on her side facing away from Liv and closed her eyes.

"I love you too, sweetie…I know…are we okay? All right, I'll call you when I can. Good night, Kim."

Sophie heard Liv toss the phone on the nightstand between the two beds before she fell back on her bed with a sigh. Sophie fought the urge to turn over.

"So how much of that did you hear? These motels have thin walls."

"I was trying not to listen," Sophie lied, finally turning onto her back and staring up at the ceiling. "I'm sorry."

"It's okay. I needed to make that call before tomorrow. If I'd known you were coming back, I'd have sat out in Justin's car to do it."

During an uncomfortable silence, Sophie struggled with whether to say anything, but in the end, her curiosity won out.

"Is Kim your daughter?" She risked a glance at the other bed. The silence stretched out so long Sophie began to wonder if Liv would answer. She was about to turn away again when Liv finally spoke.

"No. Kim's a foster kid who lives with a neighbor. I've agreed to help out when I can. She was really looking forward to going to the ball game tomorrow."

"That's nice. A lot of kids need adults to look up to." Sophie didn't know what else to say. She thought back to her own childhood and wished she'd had someone to care about her when her parents kicked her out of the house. Well, Barb did, of course, but she was family. She shuddered to think about where she might have ended up if Barb and Jay hadn't taken her in at sixteen.

"I'm trying to give her something I never had when I was her age, being bounced around from family to family," Liv said quietly. Sophie turned toward her and propped herself up on one elbow.

"You grew up in the foster system?" For some reason, that revelation surprised her, although it made sense after Frank's earlier statement about Liv wanting them to be more like a family. Liv looked at her but said nothing. Sophie had the impression Liv was sizing her up, and Sophie didn't intend to back down.

"I did," she finally admitted. Liv swung her legs over the edge of the bed and sat up. "Tell me about your childhood."

Apparently Liv's years spent growing up were off-limits. Sophie could take a hint, but she really didn't want to talk about her own upbringing either. She took a deep breath and reminded herself she needed to get along with Liv if she was going to be working on her team, even if temporarily.

"My childhood was fine until I turned sixteen and my parents threw me out of the house," she said, but stopped when Liv gave a humorless laugh. She cocked her head and looked at Liv, hoping for an elaboration.

"I'm sorry, it's just that my childhood was hell *until* I turned fifteen." Liv looked down at the floor but it quickly became obvious she wasn't going to say any more. "What did you do to piss off mommy and daddy so much? Did you come home pregnant?"

"No." Her annoyance with Liv's assumption was evident in her voice but she didn't care one little bit. How dare she presume anything about her life? "And you know what? My past is as off-limits as yours apparently is. I don't need any shit from you or anybody else, all right? I'll call Hal in the morning and let him know this arrangement isn't going to work out."

Sophie didn't wait for a response. It seemed that whenever they took one step forward, Liv pushed her about five steps back. She turned away and pulled the blankets over her head before closing her eyes to fight back tears. She hated that a virtual stranger could bring all her pain back with one thoughtless comment. When would it ever stop hurting so much?

CHAPTER NINE

He stared at the television screen in disbelief as the local news aired the footage of him taken from a convenience store. It was hard to see his face because the pictures were so grainy and he was wearing a hooded sweatshirt, but that didn't mean someone out there wouldn't recognize him. At least he hadn't grown up in the area, and no one really knew him here. There was no doubt the kid hanging onto his hand was Timmy York though.

He rubbed his sweaty palms on his pant legs and glanced over his shoulder at the door to the basement. He had to go to work. He'd put a television in the room down there so the kid wouldn't be completely bored, but he didn't like the idea of leaving him alone all day. Anything could happen, and who knew if the basement was as soundproof as he'd been told? If the kid started screaming, someone outside could hear him. At least the house was pretty much out in the middle of nowhere, so the chances of someone walking by were slim.

The other times he'd abducted kids there'd been a quick handoff, and he'd never had to hang on to any of them for more than twenty-four hours. What the hell could have happened to make the deal for this one fall through?

He went to the bathroom to shave and get ready for the job he'd gotten through a friend. He'd risk being fired if he showed up late again, but the day he dumped the Henderson girl he hadn't had much of a choice. As he looked in the mirror he saw the bruise under his left eye from where the kid had hit him the night before.

He touched it with his index finger and winced. The kid had a hell of a right cross for a five-year-old.

It scared him to think there might be something mentally wrong with this one. He'd screwed up big time with the Henderson girl. She'd been autistic, and he hadn't picked up on it beforehand. He'd been given strict orders to not take any kids who had disabilities—mental or physical.

He decided to give it a little time. Maybe Timmy was just upset at being away from his family, and it *was* his birthday. What would happen if the kid really did have something wrong? He couldn't bring himself to do what he'd done to the Henderson girl. And to that boy who he'd found out through newspaper reports had Asperger's. He'd never even heard of Asperger's before.

On the other hand, if he screwed up again he'd pay with his life. And his mother's. He couldn't let that happen. If only he hadn't been so stupid as to go to that convenience store to get the kid a bottle of chocolate milk. He didn't want to think about what might happen when that got back to the man giving him orders. He was surprised he hadn't called already.

❖

"We need to talk, Sergeant," Liv said as she followed Mansfield into his office the next morning. He looked pretty agitated, but she didn't give a damn. He had some explaining to do after the things she'd found out the night before.

"I don't have time for this," he said. "I told you Officer Parsons is your liaison with the department."

"I understand you don't like having us here," Liv said, trying to find some common ground, but he wasn't making things easy.

"That's not it at all, ma'am," he said. His expression quickly changed from agitation to obvious hatred. "We don't *need* you here. My department is perfectly capable of finding a kidnapper without your help."

"Really? That surprises me since the report concerning your initial conversation with the Yorks was so incomplete." Liv decided to dispense with the niceties. It wasn't her style, and given his attitude, she didn't want to even make an attempt. "For instance, nothing in there indicated that Peter York is not Timmy's biological father."

"I'm from this town, Agent Andrews. I'm not friends with them, but I know the Yorks and Abby's ex-husband. I'm aware Peter isn't Timmy's father. I had no reason to put that in the file," he said as he sat back with a smug smile.

"Wow, that's kind of like saying you know who the kidnapper is, so there's no reason to put his name in the file as a suspect." She watched as he suddenly found something important on his desk that needed his attention. "Do you know who the kidnapper is, Sergeant?"

"Don't be ridiculous," he said. "How the hell would I know that?"

Liv watched him in silence for a few moments and finally shook her head. He was an asshole, yes, but that didn't make him a suspect in her case.

"If you'd followed up on the bio dad—in your report—then we wouldn't have had to waste our time last night eliminating him as a suspect."

"I knew he wasn't involved, because I did follow up. He's in Florida on business."

"You knowing something doesn't help me." Liv tightened her grip on the arms of her chair in an attempt to control her growing irritation. "If you'd put it in the file, we wouldn't have had to waste our time finding out the same thing, would we?"

Liv watched Mansfield for a while, and when it became apparent he wouldn't respond, she forced herself to relax and went on.

"Timmy has disabilities too," she said. "That wasn't in the file either."

"He does?" Mansfield appeared genuinely surprised. Apparently he didn't know the Yorks as well as he thought. He shook his head. "What does that have to do with anything?"

"Kendra Henderson was kidnapped in Northampton County a week ago and found murdered four days later." Liv leaned forward in her chair. She needed to make him see the connection between the two cases, if for no other reason than to have him be a little more by the book. "She was autistic. A month ago a little boy in Monroe County was killed—he had Asperger's. We think whoever's abducting these kids doesn't want them if they're damaged. Timmy is damaged. We need to do everything in our power to find him before he ends up dead and dumped on the side of the road."

He sat quietly, studying her face. "I'm sorry, I didn't realize the cases were connected and I didn't know Timmy had problems."

Liv was surprised. She'd have thought the man would have rather chewed off his own arm than to apologize to a woman for anything.

"Well, they are. And it's possible these kidnappings are connected to others, three of whom have been killed so far." Liv stood and moved behind her chair, placing her hands on the back of it as she addressed him. "I don't want your department liaison. I want your entire department. If anyone finds out anything pertinent to the case, we need to know about it immediately. I don't need it going through two or three people before it reaches my ears, understand? We need to find some sort of middle ground so we can work together to solve this."

"Understood. You'll have the full cooperation of every one of my officers," he said. He stood and walked around the desk, his hand held out to her. "Are we good?"

"We're good," she said, shaking it.

❖

"Anything new?" Liv asked when she walked into their command center. She motioned for Sophie, who was chatting with Parsons near the front door of the station, to follow her. She really needed to have a chat with Sophie about the inappropriateness of flirting with the officer.

"He was at a convenience store with the kid early yesterday evening," Gabe said before he yawned. "The idiot at the store thought he could make a buck by selling the video to a news network instead of calling us. You can't see the man's face very well, but you can definitely tell the kid is the York boy. It's being broadcast on all the area news stations this morning, but we haven't had any calls about it yet."

"You guys go get some sleep," Liv said. She motioned for Justin to take over the computers and telephones, and tilted her head to get Sophie to follow her outside. "Can you go to the diner and get us some coffee? I need to review any notes they made overnight."

"Sure." Sophie's tone was curt and she stood with her arms folded tightly in front of her.

Liv wanted to apologize for the insensitive things she'd said the night before, but she didn't know how. Sophie hadn't said more than three words to her since they got up, and Liv had never been good with apologies. When Sophie was almost to her car, Liv jogged over to stop her, not really sure what she was doing.

"Kane," she said, with a hand on Sophie's arm. Sophie stared at the hand before meeting her eyes. Liv pulled away and looked off to her right, not wanting to see the hurt in Sophie's face. The hurt she had put there. "Look, I'm sorry about what I said last night, okay? It was thoughtless, and I really need to learn how to think before I speak. I was only trying to deflect the conversation away from me, and I truly am sorry."

Liv felt uncharacteristically awkward as she stood there letting Sophie scrutinize her. Sophie finally nodded once and then got into the car without a word. Liv watched as she drove out of the parking lot before she let out her breath. She actually wanted to scream in frustration.

"Hey, Boss," Gabe called out. She whirled and saw him jogging toward her, a piece of paper in his hand. He handed it to her and then doubled over to catch his breath. Gabe was a good fifty pounds overweight, but he'd lost about that much in the past few months. Liv examined the paper, which had a name and number on it, and the name of a school.

"What am I looking at?"

"A woman just called saying she thinks the guy in the surveillance video is a teacher at that middle school. She's the vice-principal there, and she wants to talk to you."

"Thanks, Gabe," she said before pulling out her cell phone and heading back to the building. "Go back to the motel and get a few hours of sleep. If it turns out to be a credible lead, I'll need you rested later."

"You got it."

The phone rang three times before a woman answered. Liv walked in and found Justin watching her as she spoke. She waved for Frank and Victor to go.

"Hi, this is Agent Olivia Andrews, with the FBI. I had a message that Patricia Cunningham wanted to speak with me." She waited when the woman put her on hold, not knowing if she was being transferred or hung up on, because there was only silence on the other end of the line. She looked at Justin. "Get me an address for Walton Creek Middle School."

"Hello, Agent Andrews?" an elderly woman asked a moment later.

"Yes, is this Patricia Cunningham?"

"Yes, I'm the vice-principal here. I think I know who kidnapped Timmy York."

"I was told you think it's a teacher at your school?"

"His name is Richard Kraft. He teaches seventh-grade math."

"Is he there today?" Liv motioned for Justin to hurry with the address and grabbed her jacket from the back of her chair.

"He just arrived, and his first class starts in twenty minutes."

"I'll be there as soon as I can." She closed her phone and grabbed the paper Justin held out to her.

"Is it him?" he asked.

"I don't know, but why would a co-worker be turning him in without a good reason? Call Sophie's cell and tell her to meet me there. You stay here and I'll let you know when we finish interviewing him."

Chapter Ten

Patricia Cunningham was waiting on the front steps with Sophie by her side when Liv pulled into a space near the entrance and jumped out.

"I can show you where his classroom is," she offered once the introductions were out of the way. She started toward the entrance, but Liv stopped her.

"Mrs. Cunningham, we'd like to speak with you first, if you don't mind."

The woman nodded before leading them inside and down a hall to her office. Once they were there, she shut the door and they all took seats.

"I'm curious as to why you think Mr. Kraft is the man we're looking for," Liv said.

"Richard has always been a good teacher," Mrs. Cunningham said. It appeared as though it pained her to be accusing a colleague of something so serious, which intensified Liv's hope that they had the right guy. "He's been teaching here for about three years and has always been such a nice man. But lately he's been acting rather strange. He's been coming to work late quite often, and recently he always seems to be distracted."

"When did his behavior change?" Sophie asked. Liv relaxed back into her chair and allowed Sophie to take the lead. She used the time to study Mrs. Cunningham.

She was probably in her mid-sixties, and her gray hair was pulled back in a tight bun. Her light-blue eyes clearly didn't miss a thing, and Liv got caught staring more than once. After the second time, she looked down at what Sophie was writing. Her heart sank a bit at the words she read.

"He's only been acting strange for a few days?" she asked, redirecting her gaze to the vice-principal. If that was true, Kraft probably wasn't their man. The hopeless feeling from the Henderson case crowded back into her mind, but she shook her head with the hope she could keep it at bay for a while longer.

"A little less than a week, yes. He came in this past Tuesday and was very fidgety. By midday he was sweating profusely, and we sent him home, concerned he might have something contagious. He came back the next day decidedly feeling better, but he was as nervous as a cat in a room full of rocking chairs, if you'll pardon the cliché. Every little noise seemed to set him off, and he was constantly looking out the windows as though he expected someone to be coming after him. When I saw that man on the television, well, he's the same size and it just looked like him."

"I think we're ready to see Mr. Kraft now, if you'd be so kind as to get him for us," Sophie said after Liv gave her a nod.

"Should I have him come in here?" Mrs. Cunningham asked.

"If you wouldn't mind." Liv took Sophie's notebook away from her to study it.

"What are you thinking?" Sophie asked when they were alone.

Liv was silent for a moment as she read through the notes again. He *could* be their guy, but she had her doubts. Something just didn't feel right.

"Tuesday was the day we found Kendra Henderson's body," she finally said with a sigh.

"So he was just nervous something would lead us back to him." Sophie sounded sure, and Liv met her eyes. It made sense he'd be nervous, but why would that have been the first day?

"The medical examiner said her body was dumped Monday night, but she wasn't killed there. Not only that, but she was dead for three days before we found her. *If* he's the guy we're looking for, I would think he'd have been acting strange when he actually killed her, not just the day the body was discovered." Liv went to look out the window behind the desk.

"Unless he was experienced," Sophie said, crossing her arms over her chest.

"But if he was experienced, then he probably wouldn't have been nervous at all, body or no body," Liv said without looking at her. "And if this is related to the Henderson case, then I highly doubt he'd turn around and grab a kid from his own town, where the people here know him."

"So you don't think Kraft is our guy?"

"I want it to be him as much as you do, but my gut tells me no. Maybe my opinion of him will change once we have a chance to speak with him." As she turned to go back to her seat the door opened, and Mrs. Cunningham entered behind a man in his thirties who looked like he was high on something. His eyes darted around the room, flicking over everything but her and Sophie. The vice-principal made the introductions, and when Liv flashed her ID at him, Richard Kraft sat down hard, staring at her as though she were a ghost.

"Would you excuse us, please?" Liv asked Mrs. Cunningham. The woman nodded and left the room, closing the door behind her. Liv turned her attention to Kraft.

"What's going on?" he asked quietly.

"We just have a few questions for you, Mr. Kraft," Sophie said.

He wiped his palms brusquely on the legs of his slacks and looked quickly from Sophie to her and back again. He nodded and Sophie glanced at her notes.

"Okay," he said, sounding apprehensive.

"Can you tell us where you were last Monday evening?" Sophie asked.

"What was the date?" Kraft glanced out the window behind Liv before turning his attention to his hands in his lap.

Liv recognized the tactic. He was stalling—desperately trying to come up with an answer they would believe.

"It would have been the fourth," she said.

"I was at home with my wife," he said quickly, never raising his eyes.

"We'll need a phone number so we can verify that with her." She propped herself against the desk and folded her arms in front of her chest. He refused to look at her.

"Did you know Kendra Henderson?" Sophie asked. Liv thought she saw Kraft flinch at the mention of the girl's name, but he looked at Sophie.

"The little girl they found dead a few days ago?" When Sophie nodded, he shook his head. "Only what I read in the paper. It was horrible."

"Do you know Timmy York?" Liv asked. He finally looked at her, and with what she assumed was a show of bravado, he held her gaze.

"Most of the people in Walton Creek know Timmy, at least enough to say hello. His stepfather owns the diner in the center of town." He was silent for a moment, and apparently the real reason for their visit began to dawn on him. His face turned a shade of red Liv had never seen before. "Is that what this is about? You think I did it?"

"You do bear a resemblance to the man in the surveillance footage," Sophie said quietly. "We need to be able to rule you out as a suspect at this point."

"I would never hurt a child. My wife and I are trying to get pregnant. I love kids. If I didn't, I wouldn't be a teacher."

"How long have you been teaching, Mr. Kraft?" Liv asked.

"I started here three years ago."

"And before that?"

"In Philadelphia."

"Why the move up here?" Sophie asked. Liv glanced at her, pleasantly surprised they seemed to be on the same wavelength. "Do you have relatives in the area?"

"My wife and I thought it would be a better place to raise kids," he said with another glance out the window. "Apparently that isn't the case though, is it?"

"We're going to need names and phone numbers of your previous employers as well as your wife, Mr. Kraft. Believe me, we want to clear you as quickly as possible so we can move on with our investigation," Sophie said with a forced smile. Obviously Sophie wasn't convinced Kraft *wasn't* their guy.

"Are we done here?" Kraft asked as he stood and headed for the door.

"No, we're not. I have a few more questions," Liv said. His shoulders sagged before he turned back around. She pointed at a spot just below his left eye. "Where'd you get the bruise?"

At her question, he put his fingers to the spot and winced slightly. It wasn't a big bruise, and in fact she hadn't even noticed it until he'd turned away and the light caught it. The color indicated it was fairly new, though, and with what they'd learned about Timmy York's anger issues, it was a little too coincidental. God, she hoped Richard Kraft was their suspect.

"I coach Little League. I got hit with a foul ball yesterday afternoon."

"It's not very warm in here, Mr. Kraft, but you're sweating an awful lot. Why is that?" Liv pushed away from the desk and took a step toward him. He stood up straighter and looked her in the eye.

"I have back problems. The doctor put me on a new medication, and I seem to be having an adverse reaction to it."

"You have an answer for everything, don't you, Mr. Kraft?" she asked. She motioned for Sophie to hand her the notebook she'd been writing in and turned it to a clean page before shoving it at him. "I need you to give us your previous employer's name and number, your wife's, and your doctor's."

She stood in front of him as he wrote all the requested information down. His hands shook, and he wiped the sweat from his brow more than once. When he handed it back to Liv, she glanced at it before putting it in her pocket.

"If you are involved in the death of Kendra Henderson and the disappearance of Timmy York, we will find out, Mr. Kraft." Liv smiled when he backed away from her. "It's only a matter of time."

CHAPTER ELEVEN

The wife corroborated his story," Justin said when he walked into the office a couple of hours later. He looked as disappointed as Liv felt.

"So did the doctor," Sophie added as she hung up the phone, "except according to him, Kraft has been taking this particular medication for a few months now and has never complained about it. The possible side effects he described to me are the same things Mrs. Cunningham mentioned and the things we saw while we were talking to him. However, the doctor does think it's a bit strange Kraft hadn't mentioned them when he saw him about three weeks ago."

"All right, so the wife could be lying to protect her husband, because based on what the doctor told you, and what I found out from Kraft's assistant Little League coach, I'm beginning to think that maybe he *is* involved in this somehow." Liv sat back in her chair and put her feet up on the table.

"What did you find out?" Justin asked. Liv smiled at the way she had his full attention. He was always so eager when there was a new lead to work. She used to be that way too—before the kids started turning up dead.

"He was not hit by a foul ball in practice yesterday like he told us, and the assistant coach doesn't remember seeing a bruise under Kraft's eye." Liv stared up at the ceiling. "In fact, for most of the practice, he sat in his car talking on his cell phone. But he was there from just before three until just after five. According to Sergeant

Friendly's notes, the abduction happened sometime between three and three thirty. The witness who saw the man walking away from the park with a little boy says it was about ten after three. Kraft definitely can't be our kidnapper, but that doesn't mean he didn't have someone else take the boy and deliver him later in the evening."

"If Mansfield catches wind of you calling him Sergeant Friendly he won't be very happy," Justin said, trying to suppress a grin.

"A man like that won't ever be happy, no matter what. Especially when a woman's in charge of this investigation," Sophie said, and looked at Liv. "Are we going to put a tail on Kraft?"

"Already done." Liv smiled and put her feet back on the ground. She stood up and took a deep breath. "And Sergeant Friendly isn't happy about having to coordinate a stakeout."

Sophie sat at the bar and ordered a beer. While she waited for it, she looked around the dive and suppressed a shudder. The place was filthy and smelled like stale beer and cigarettes, but that didn't seem to deter the locals from showing up in droves. It was a Friday night, though, which would explain the crowd.

The bartender put a bottle in front of her as he handed her a menu encased in plastic and covered in something sticky. She didn't even want to think about what it might be. She'd been surprised when Liv asked her to join her for dinner. Sophie wasn't about to reject the attempt at bridging the gap between them, so she decided to wait for Liv, though no way in hell would she eat anything that came out of the bar's kitchen. As long as they were stuck in this town, she'd be perfectly happy to eat every meal at the diner down the street from the motel. Hell, she'd even drive the twenty minutes into Allentown to find something else.

She glanced at the door every time it opened, beginning to worry Liv wouldn't show. Convincing herself something must have broken with the case, she slapped down a five-dollar bill and stood to leave. At that very moment Liv walked through the door, and a rather large man stepped between them. His grin was missing more than a few teeth, and his greasy, stringy hair gave Sophie the heebie-jeebies. She tried to ignore her revulsion and attempted to push past him, but he put an arm out to stop her.

"Hey there, pretty lady, you just got here. You ain't leavin' already, are ya?"

"Excuse me," she said, turning her head from the stench emanating from his mouth. He grabbed her arm and held her in place. She met his eyes with a gaze she hoped was steely, and after a moment he let go, holding his hands up in the air.

"No disrespect, ma'am. Just wanted to buy ya a drink."

"No, thank you." Sophie saw Liv hanging back by the door watching. She appeared to find the situation amusing. "I'm not interested."

"Well, if ya change your mind, I'll be right over here at the pool table with my buddies."

The man walked away without another word, and Sophie glared at Liv, who was laughing as she strode toward her and took the seat next to her. She couldn't stop the shudder that ran through her body, relief washing over her at the realization of just how close she'd come to being completely trapped by Bubba.

"I'm glad you think it was funny." She picked up her beer and watched Bubba with his buddies in the mirror behind the bar. "You know, you could have walked over here and helped me out."

Sophie took a pull from her beer but felt Liv's eyes on her, studying her. She liked the thought of Liv scrutinizing her so closely. Her cheeks flushed and she looked away.

"Honestly, you don't strike me as the kind of woman who needs rescuing, Agent Kane," Liv said, sounding as though the notion might actually surprise her. "And judging by the way he turned tail and ran, I'd say I was spot-on with my assessment."

"I don't need rescuing." Sophie picked at the label on her beer. "But that doesn't mean I wouldn't appreciate some help now and again."

"Duly noted." Liv ducked her head before ordering a beer. "Smart move to order something in a bottle. I'd be afraid to drink anything from this place out of a glass."

"Speaking of which, are you seriously going to eat dinner here? I'd rather stop at the diner on the way back to the motel, if it's all the same to you," Sophie said. She picked up the menu and handed it to Liv. "Check this out."

She laughed when Liv crinkled her nose at the sticky substance on it and dropped it on the bar before using the condensation on her bottle to clean the mess off her fingers.

"The diner's fine," Liv said, rubbing her hands on her thighs.

They were silent for a few moments, but Sophie was hyper-aware of every time Liv turned her head to look at her as though she might say something. After the third time, Sophie faced her.

"Do you want to talk about something?"

Liv shook her head and took a drink of her beer. Sophie continued to watch her, but she refused to look in her direction again and stayed stubbornly silent.

"If we're going to share a room, there are some things we should know about each other," she said. While Liv's appearance led her to believe she was a lesbian, Sophie had learned over the years to not judge a person based solely on how they looked. Liv looked at her expectantly, and just as she was about to say something, Liv beat her to it.

"Are you married?"

"Excuse me?" Sophie asked, caught off guard by the one question she hadn't expected.

"Are you married?" Liv repeated.

"No."

"In a relationship?"

"Are you asking because you're interested, Agent Andrews?" Sophie couldn't stop the grin at the sight of Liv's cheeks turning red. The lighting in the bar wasn't so dark that it escaped her notice, but she decided to take pity on her. "Why don't you just ask what you want to know?"

Liv looked at her for a while, then finished off what was left in her bottle before standing. She took a deep breath and met Sophie's eyes.

"I'm a lesbian, Agent Kane. If that's a problem for you and you haven't called Hal yet, I'll do it first thing in the morning and ask to have you removed from my team."

Before Sophie could even think to react, Liv had turned and was walking out of the bar. She grabbed her jacket and hurried after her.

"Liv, wait," she said as she caught up with her and placed a hand on her shoulder. Liv turned around to face her, and Sophie noticed for the first time just how guarded Liv was. She could see it in the weariness of her beautiful green eyes and in the hard set of her jaw. Sophie ached to take away whatever pain Liv had suffered in her life, but she hadn't a clue how to go about it. Or even if Liv would welcome such an attempt. Or why the hell she'd actually want to. But she decided right then and there that it was her mission to get Liv to open up. She'd worry about her reasons later.

"I'm sorry. I shouldn't have pushed you. I was only kidding around. It doesn't bother me that you're a lesbian. In fact, I am too. And I really wish you wouldn't call Hal just yet. I'm invested in the case, and I'd like to see it through, if it's all the same to you."

"I don't have a problem if you don't. But I do need to discuss something with you if you really want to stick it out." Liv pulled her keys out of her pocket. "I don't like what I'm seeing between you and Parsons. We're here to work, not to fraternize with the local law enforcement."

"I don't know what you think you see going on, Liv, but I am not fraternizing with anyone." Sophie shook her head as she spoke. "I'll make sure she knows I'm not interested, if that'll make you feel better."

Liv just stared at her, not knowing how to respond. Letting her stay on the team was a bad idea, especially since she was becoming attracted to Sophie.

"It isn't about making me feel better," Liv said, even though that wasn't true. "It could be a distraction, and a conflict of interest."

"I'll take care of it. And thanks for trusting me enough to tell me you're a lesbian. I know firsthand it's not always an easy thing to let people know."

"I'm sorry I just put it out there like that, but I prefer to let everyone know up front, because I've had problems about it in the past."

"I'd like to hear about it if you want to talk to me," Sophie said, and for a moment Liv considered it. But she didn't know Sophie, and there were things she'd never told anyone but Justin.

"Maybe someday, but not tonight, all right?" she said.

"Seriously?" Sophie asked after an awkward silence. "You thought I was straight?"

Liv shrugged indifferently and turned to get into her SUV.

"Please tell me you at least *hoped* I was a lesbian."

"We're not having this conversation, Kane," Liv said, keeping her expression neutral. "If you want dinner, then follow me to the diner."

Hoped she was a lesbian? God, yes, but Liv could never admit it to Sophie. There was a definite attraction between them, and Liv had to fight it. But the feeling of wanting to open up to someone was new, and she wasn't entirely sure she liked it.

She'd always kept her thoughts and feelings to herself, but something about Sophie had her wanting to bare her soul. That wasn't possible, and she had to keep her distance. Sophie had been flirting with her, and while it felt good, it could only lead to trouble. The kind of trouble she wasn't ready to deal with.

CHAPTER TWELVE

Four days and no new leads later, Liv, Sophie, and Justin walked into the station to be greeted with a rendition of "Happy birthday to you" by Gabe, Victor, and Frank.

Liv wanted to smile because this family of hers had remembered her birthday, but the case was dragging her down. She'd discussed it with Hal at length the night before, and since there were no leads to follow up, they agreed that two of the team members would take a couple of days off and go back home. When they returned, two others would go. That would continue until something broke in the case or—the scenario none of them wanted—until Timmy turned up dead. Liv was desperately hoping it wouldn't happen that way because it had been nearly a week since he'd disappeared.

"Thanks, guys," she said, sitting down in the chair they ushered her in to. She shook her head when Officer Parsons walked in with a cupcake, complete with a lighted candle. Liv sat through the group singing to her again and dutifully blew out the candle before catching Parsons's eye. "How'd they manage to recruit you to participate?"

"It wasn't a problem," Beth said, with a glance at Sophie. Liv looked at Sophie too, who seemed oblivious to the young officer's attentions.

"I see," Liv said, and Beth stood a bit straighter and looked Liv in the eye. At least Parsons was now aware Liv knew about the attraction. Maybe she'd get the hint and back off.

"Happy birthday, Liv," Sophie said, with a smile that warmed Liv. She couldn't help but smile back.

"Thank you." Liv had avoided being alone with her over the past few days, because she was embarrassed about what had happened that night in the bar. Hal's insistence that Sophie take her two days off with Liv would be interesting though. They would drive home in separate cars, but it was silly for them to drive back up separately. She wasn't looking forward to the long ride back to Walton Creek from Philadelphia.

"This is ridiculous, Agent Andrews," Mansfield said as he charged into the room, effectively ending the birthday celebration. Parsons scurried past him and back out to her desk. "I can't keep someone tailing Kraft everywhere indefinitely. The man obviously isn't involved, because he hasn't done anything out of the ordinary."

"Maybe he knows you're following him and is being overly cautious."

"Are you insinuating I don't know how to run a stakeout?" he asked, with more than a hint of a challenge. She sighed when she met his eyes. She'd known it was too good to be true when they'd agreed on a sort of truce.

"I'm not insinuating anything, Sergeant, but should I be worried about your abilities in that area?" She did her best to keep calm, but Mansfield really rubbed her the wrong way. She tried not to let her frustration with the case show, but realized it was apparent in her demeanor. Not only had Kraft been on his best behavior since they'd been to see him last Friday, but there hadn't been any new leads to speak of. They didn't have enough to get a search warrant for his house either. Between the six of them on the team, they'd spoken with everyone in town at least twice, and nothing seemed out of the ordinary. It was like the damn kid had simply vanished into thin air. "Who's tailing him now?"

"My overnight officer, Winters," he answered, wisely choosing to ignore her barb.

"Keep after him for a few more days. If the York kid turns up dead and Kraft still hasn't done anything out of the ordinary, we'll pull the surveillance." She stood and gathered her things, not looking at him as she continued to speak. "Two of us will be leaving for home. We'll be on a rotating schedule so four agents will be here at all times. If something breaks in the case, we all live close enough that we can be back here in no more than two hours."

Mansfield mumbled something under his breath Liv couldn't quite catch. She straightened and faced him. Mansfield took a step back, apparently still not comfortable with her height advantage.

"Is there a problem, Sergeant? Because a few days ago you told me you didn't need us here at all. That you were perfectly capable of catching our kidnapper on your own. Unless you haven't told me something?"

Mansfield looked away from her and shook his head before stalking out of the room. Liv returned to what she was doing, fighting hard to not say something sarcastic. As much as she hated leaving her team with Mansfield around, she knew it was time to take a break.

"You heading out now?" Justin asked when Mansfield was out of earshot.

"Sophie and I are going home. We'll be back Thursday night, and then you and Gabe can go Friday morning."

"No problem." He walked over to her, lowering his voice so no one else in the room could hear him. "You look exhausted. I hope you'll get some rest while you're home."

"I will. But I'm also taking Kim to a baseball game. I hate to disappoint her like I did."

"Good. Maybe you should take Kane along too." He chuckled when Liv shot him a look of consternation. "Relax. I just think if you get to know her better you might really like her. She seems like a good person."

"Don't push it, Ingram," she said sternly. "I don't need a matchmaker."

❖

In spite of Liv's reaction to Justin's suggestion, she found herself standing at the box office of Citizens Bank Park later that day intending to buy three tickets to the next night's game. She hadn't asked Sophie if she wanted to go, and as she waited in line she argued with herself about whether she would actually purchase three tickets or two. She pulled her phone out and scrolled down to Sophie's number but stopped just short of pushing the call button.

She couldn't figure out what about Sophie had her questioning everything about herself. She'd never felt the need to talk about her past with anyone, yet Sophie had a way of making her want to open up. Sophie seemed interested in more than a working relationship, if her mild flirtation was any indication. The questions she asked about Liv's life seemed genuine, and she felt certain Sophie wanted, at the very least, a friendship. The problem was Liv and her hard-and-fast rule of not getting involved with anyone she worked with. The way Sophie looked at her sometimes made her rethink her personal policies on that front though. She shook her head and glanced at her phone once more before putting it back in her pocket. It would be stupid to spend time with Sophie outside of the investigation. As she stepped up to the window, she kept repeating to herself, "Two tickets, two tickets."

"Can I help you?" the woman on the other side of the glass asked.

"I need three tickets for tomorrow night's game."

❖

"You have three tickets here," Kim said when Liv handed the envelope to her later that evening. She narrowed her eyes as she studied Liv's face. "You aren't bringing Emily, are you?"

"No. She and I had an argument the night I left to work on this case, and, well, we aren't seeing each other anymore." Liv had wondered briefly that afternoon if she should call Emily and invite her instead of Sophie, but she didn't want to. She hadn't even thought about Emily since the night she left. Besides, Kim and Em seriously disliked each other. That made the decision even easier. She tried to ignore the look of happiness on Kim's face her words seemed to evoke. "I was thinking about inviting along a new agent on my team."

"Is she nice?" Kim accepted the can of soda Liv handed her but never took her eyes from Liv's face, her smile way too knowing for a girl her age.

"What makes you think it's a she?" Liv smiled back, marveling at the kid's proverbial steel-trap mind.

"Because if it wasn't, you wouldn't be so nervous about asking her."

Liv stared at her for a moment before holding her hand out. "I want to see your identification. I don't believe you're only thirteen. You may have everyone else fooled with your act, but not me."

Kim laughed, and Liv realized how much she liked Kim to be happy. It didn't happen nearly often enough.

"What's her name?"

"Sophie Kane."

"Is she cute?"

"Stop," Liv said, trying to sound stern, but Sophie's face crowded its way into her thoughts. *Adorable,* she wanted to say. *Gorgeous, even.* "She's too old for you."

Kim's face turned serious much too fast for Liv's liking. She watched as Kim turned her attention to the soda can in front of her. Liv sat at the kitchen table next to her and waited, knowing Kim wanted to say something but needed to work up the nerve to do it.

"You think I'm gay?" she finally asked. Liv struggled with how to respond. She wished to God she'd had someone to talk to about what she was going through when she was Kim's age.

"I don't know whether you are or not, Kim. You're the only one who can answer that question, but I want you to know I'm here for you either way, all right?" Liv spoke quietly, and Kim refused to look at her. "No matter what, I'll *always* be here for you. You can talk to me about anything, you know that, right?"

Kim nodded and took a sip from her can. Liv wiped the tear from Kim's cheek before Kim turned her head away. Liv fought back tears of her own at the memory of how it felt to believe you were truly alone in the world. She would give anything for Kim not to feel that way.

"You should call her and ask if she wants to go."

Liv was jolted out of her thoughts and tried to catch up with the sudden change of subject.

"What?"

"Call her and ask," Kim repeated. She picked Liv's cell phone up and held it out to her. When Liv didn't immediately take it, Kim smiled and pushed the button to turn the display on. "If you don't, then I will. I don't think you want me calling her though."

Liv came to her senses and grabbed the phone. She shook her head to accompany the warning look she gave Kim, but couldn't help smiling at Kim's innocent expression.

"You can be really evil sometimes," she said before finding Sophie's number and calling. "I won't forget this."

Kim's smile of satisfaction lightened Liv's heart a bit, but then it began to thud heavily when Sophie answered. She walked to the other side of the room.

"Hi, Sophie, it's Liv."

"Has something happened with the case? I can be ready to leave in five minutes."

"Slow down, I'm not calling about the case." She glanced over her shoulder and rolled her eyes when she saw Kim had moved into the living room to be closer so she could hear the conversation. "I was calling to see if you were busy tomorrow night."

There was silence on the other end of the line, and Liv glanced at the phone's display to make sure the call hadn't been dropped.

"Are you asking me out?" Sophie sounded doubtful, and a little nervous, which actually helped Liv relax a bit.

"No, Kane, I'm asking you if you would like to accompany us to a baseball game."

"Us?"

"Kim and me. You remember who Kim is, right?"

"Yes, and I'd love to go." She couldn't be sure, but she thought Sophie sounded happy at the prospect. "Where should I meet you?"

"At the park—" Kim waved her arms and shook her head adamantly. "Actually, I can pick you up at your place around five, if that's all right."

Kim relaxed back into the couch with a smug expression while Liv wrote down the address and finished her call. After hanging up, she pointed at Kim but couldn't keep a straight face.

"You are a piece of work, young lady," she said.

❖

Liv was getting ready to go to bed when her phone rang. She glanced at the clock, hoping it was her parents, who had never forgotten her birthday before. She smiled when she heard her mother's voice on the other end of the line.

"You thought we forgot, didn't you?" Janet Andrews asked, her tone playful. "Kyle, she thought we forgot."

"No, I didn't," Liv said with a chuckle. "How are things in the Windy City?"

"Oh, you know how it is," Janet said. "There's no shortage of sick people, so your father will always have work. And as long as people keep having babies, I'll still be teaching. How are things there?"

"I'm in the middle of a case." They spoke on the phone at least once a week, but she never really went into details about the cases she worked.

"It's a bad one?"

"Aren't they all when you're talking about abducted children?" She sat down on the edge of her bed and bent forward, her elbows on her knees. "Sometimes I wonder why I do this shit."

"Because you care, honey. Where would the world be without people who care?"

Liv smiled and stretched out on the bed. Her mother always had such a simplistic way of looking at things. But she was right, and Liv knew it. She did care. She cared about all those kids who had parents who loved them, and it broke her heart when some sick fuck took them away.

"Have you talked to Cindy lately?" her mother asked. She sounded guarded, which worried her.

"No, I haven't. Why?"

"The news reported that her appeal was denied. I thought she would have called you when that happened. She always seems to call you when she needs help."

Liv closed her eyes and said a little prayer for her old friend. She wasn't much for praying but decided it couldn't hurt. Sometimes she thought Cindy was only in her life to give her a little perspective. So she could see what might have happened to her if the Andrewses hadn't come along and saved her.

"What about her kids?"

"They were put back into the system. Are you going to help her out?"

"I can't, Mom," Liv said, more weary now than she'd been an hour earlier. She'd tried to help Cindy when she'd gotten into trouble in the past and failed. She just continued to break the law no matter how many times Liv tried to put her on a different path. "I have more important things to deal with right now. We're on opposite sides of the law, and the sooner I get that through my head, the sooner I'll be able to break free of it. Besides, being convicted of first-degree murder and having an appeal denied—she's beyond help now."

Thankfully her mother changed the subject and they talked for a few more minutes. Before they hung up Liv promised to call them when she finished the case. Liv turned out the light and sat there in the dark, wondering where things had gone so wrong for Cindy. They'd promised to be friends forever when they were removed from the Calhouns' house. She'd tried, but Cindy seemed determined to fuck up her life at every turn. Liv had spent too many years rushing to her aid, and she refused to do it anymore. She hated that it had taken her so many years to realize their friendship was one-sided, which made her even more determined to help Kim. She didn't want Kim to turn out like Cindy. The Andrewses had given her an opportunity, and she wanted to do everything in her power to do the same for Kim.

CHAPTER THIRTEEN

Sophie had been looking forward to the game ever since Liv had called her the night before. She'd tried her best to engage Kim in conversation throughout the car ride to the park, but the girl would give only one-word answers, most of which sounded like grunts. She was determined to get the girl to open up before the night was over, and she promised herself Kim's surly attitude wouldn't stand in her way of enjoying a night out with Liv, away from their investigation.

"God, can you smell that?" Liv asked when they settled in their seats. Sophie bent forward to look at her around Kim, who had the seat between them.

"What?"

"The smell of the ballpark in early April," Kim said. She rolled her eyes and spoke in a tone that indicated she'd heard that phrase from Liv many times. "There's only one thing better than the smell of the ballpark in early April."

"And what's that?" Sophie asked. She smiled at the way Liv playfully pushed against Kim's shoulder.

"The smell of the ballpark in late October," Liv said.

"You know why, right?" Kim looked at her from the corner of her eye, and Sophie had the feeling Kim was testing her.

"Of course I do. The playoffs and World Series are in October." Sophie sat back in her seat with a satisfied grin as she spoke, but she didn't miss the way Kim elbowed Liv's side. She closed her eyes and breathed deeply, letting the familiar smells transport her back to her childhood, when she was still the apple of her father's eye and he would take her to the ball games every weekend. She felt a stab of regret for what she'd lost, but she wouldn't change a thing about how she'd lived her life.

"Sophie," Liv said.

"I'm sorry, what did you say?" Sophie flushed, aware she'd been lost in her memories.

"I asked if you wanted a beer or something." Liv was looking at her with concern, and Sophie wondered how long she'd been trying to get her attention.

"That would be great." She reached into her pocket to get money, but Liv got up and walked out of the row on the other side without a word. "I was going to pay for it."

"She wouldn't let you anyway," Kim said. Sophie looked at her, surprised Kim would say something without prompting. Kim got up and moved to Liv's seat but then looked at Sophie with a smile. "She's single. Just in case you were wondering."

"Are you trying to play matchmaker?"

"I'm just saying." Kim shrugged and pulled her hood over her head before turning to watch the Phillies take the field.

Sophie sat back and looked at the field too, but she wasn't seeing much. Was Liv attracted to her? She shook her head. Even if she was, she wouldn't have discussed it with a teenager, would she? Maybe Kim was just trying to push Liv into dating. Either way, it didn't matter, because Sophie wasn't looking. And even if she was, she wouldn't consider someone she worked with. That felt incestuous somehow. She suppressed a shiver when she felt Kim's eyes on her again.

"You're single, right?" Kim asked suddenly.

"I am," Sophie admitted. "And I like it that way."

"You're a lot more attractive than Emily."

"Who?"

"Liv's ex. She hated me hanging around." Kim looked sad. "I'm glad they aren't seeing each other anymore."

"How long ago did they break up?" Sophie inwardly cringed because it wasn't any of her business, but she couldn't help being curious.

"When Liv left to work your new case. Emily could never understand why Liv's job was so important to her." Kim returned her attention to the field, where the first batter was getting ready.

Sophie was surprised to learn she and Liv seemed to have something in common. None of Sophie's exes ever understood her job either. It might be a great way to open up a dialogue for things other than work, but Sophie couldn't get over the fact she was attracted to Liv.

Even more so after seeing the tender side of Liv as she interacted with Kim. It was a stark contrast to the first time they'd met, when Liv had been standoffish and left Sophie on her own to introduce herself to the majority of the team. Liv Andrews was a puzzle Sophie was intent on solving.

"Thank you for a wonderful evening," Sophie said when Liv pulled up outside her apartment building. Sophie reached for the door handle but then stopped. "Would you like to come in for a drink?"

Liv's heart lurched. It was an innocent-enough suggestion, and Liv was silently kicking herself for having dropped Kim off first. But it was a school night, and it was on the way to Sophie's from the ballpark. It had made sense at the time. She didn't have any reason to say no to Sophie's offer, so before she knew what was happening, she found herself walking into Sophie's apartment behind her. She closed the door while Sophie walked to the kitchen and opened the fridge.

"What would you like?"

"Whatever you're having is fine," she said as she sat on the oversized leather sofa. Sophie handed her a bottle of water before taking a seat at the opposite end.

"It was a great game, wasn't it?" Sophie asked, her feet propped up on the coffee table and one arm stretched along the back of the couch.

"It was." Liv took a drink of her water. "I'm sorry if Kim was a bit standoffish. It takes a while for her to open up to new people."

Sophie laughed, and Liv wondered what she'd said to cause such a reaction.

"Kim was actually quite talkative when you went to get food or drinks." Sophie looked at her and laughed again at what Liv knew was her shocked expression. "She made sure I knew beyond a shadow of a doubt about your relationship status."

"What did she say?" Liv's throat was dry, and she downed the rest of the water quickly. *I'm going to kill that kid.*

"Only that you broke up with your last girlfriend the day Timmy York was abducted. She must have told me five times that you're single."

"I'm so sorry." Liv's face got warm and she was mortified to realize she was blushing.

"Unless you instructed her to say those things, you have nothing to be sorry for, Liv. She cares about you, and after watching the two of you together for a few hours, it's pretty obvious you care a great deal for her too. She's just looking out for you."

"Still…" A long silence ensued. It wasn't entirely comfortable, and Liv was trying to think of a way to escape. She didn't realize she'd been rubbing her shoulder until she felt Sophie slide across the couch and push her hands away to massage it for her. Liv was suddenly aware of how close Sophie was. Her leg burned where their thighs were touching but she didn't move. She wasn't sure she could have even if she'd wanted to. Liv took a deep breath and the scent of Sophie's cologne, which had been teasing her all evening, hit her full force. The musk with a hint of spice went perfectly with Sophie's own scent.

"Your muscles are really tight, Liv," she said quietly. Liv's heart raced as she considered feigning nausea so she could get back to her own apartment, but the hands on either side of her neck felt too good. "Do you have headaches often?"

"Yes." She grunted, trying hard not to groan in appreciation of Sophie's soft, strong hands kneading out the knots.

"You need to learn how to relax," Sophie said, her fingers performing magic on Liv's tired muscles. "You carry all your stress in your neck and shoulders."

Liv wanted to make her stop, she really did. Alarm bells were clanging a warning in her head, but she ignored them and concentrated solely on the feel of Sophie's hands working the tension out. Her head slowly moved backward and stopped only when it hit Sophie's shoulder. Sophie's fingers stroked her cheek gently, and Liv tried to tell herself to put a stop to it. Instead, she leaned into the touch, and before she was fully aware of what was happening, Sophie stood there before her, pulling her up to a standing position.

"You're so beautiful, Liv."

Liv couldn't deny her own arousal when she saw the desire dancing in Sophie's eyes. Everything in her brain was screaming at her to stop what was happening, but an invisible force seemed to pull them together. Before she could think of a plausible way to run away from the situation, Sophie's next words brought her back from the brink.

"I really want to kiss you right now."

Liv cupped Sophie's face in her hands and moved closer, gently touching her lips to Sophie's. When Sophie's arms went around her neck, pulling her closer, Liv groaned. Sophie's lips parted, and Liv eagerly deepened the kiss. Nothing else existed but the two of them and the arousal taking over her body. Sophie moaned into her mouth and Liv pulled Sophie's thigh up to circle her waist. Sophie complied by pulling herself up so both legs were wrapped around Liv, and Liv's hands were holding her up by her ass. Sophie began to thrust against Liv and pulled away to break their kiss.

"Please, Liv, bedroom. Now."

Sophie felt the disconnection between them as though someone had slapped her. Breathing heavily, Liv seemed to come to her senses, and Sophie shook her head even as Liv was setting her on her feet and backing away from her, definite fear in her eyes.

"I'm sorry," Liv said softly. "That never should have happened."

"Liv, please talk to me." She could feel Liv slipping away from her and knew she couldn't do anything to stop her. She reached for her arm, but Liv pulled away as though she might get burned.

"I should go." She walked toward the door but stopped and turned back. "I'll call Hal tomorrow morning. I really don't think you being on my team is going to work out."

Sophie stood there in silence long after Liv shut the door.

"Damn it," she said under her breath. Liv was attractive, yes, and experiencing how tender she was with Kim had been a stark contrast to the Liv Andrews she'd seen in Walton Creek. But no matter how bad she wanted her, Liv was right. It couldn't happen. Maybe when the case was over and she was back to her training for hostage negotiation, but certainly not now. How many times had she wished she could meet someone who would understand the demands of her job? She was pretty certain getting involved with her direct superior was not a good idea, and it was sorely evident Liv felt the same way. Even so, she refused to let Liv have her taken off the team now. She was deeply invested in the case and could control her attraction, couldn't she?

CHAPTER FOURTEEN

W hat did you say?" Liv was incredulous. She'd waited until she knew Hal would be in the office, but apparently Sophie didn't have that kind of decorum.

"I said Sophie already called me," Hal told her once again. He sounded perturbed, which irritated her. "She told me you'd be calling this morning, but she wanted to make sure I knew what happened between the two of you was nothing but a misunderstanding. She wants to stay on your team, Andrews, and frankly, I don't think it's a good idea to remove her in the middle of an ongoing investigation. So I suggest the two of you work together to resolve whatever your conflict is."

"Un-fucking-believable," she muttered. She'd tossed and turned all night thinking about—and dreading—calling Hal, and she'd almost made herself sick about it. She was definitely attracted to Sophie, and the only way to fight her feelings was to have her disappear. The entire situation would end badly. She never should have invited her to that damn baseball game. "Did she tell you what happened?"

"No. She just said you'd had a misunderstanding." He paused, and Liv knew he was thinking the worst. "Andrews, is something going on I need to know about?"

"No, sir." She wanted to wring someone's neck. No, that didn't begin to describe how she was feeling. She wanted to wring *Sophie's* neck.

"What's the problem, Liv?" Hal asked after a moment. "Is there really no way the two of you can get through whatever this is? I know you can be a bit difficult to work with, but surely you can see past your differences. Or is it something on a more personal level?"

"No, it's not what you're thinking," she said, even though it was. She was trying not to lash out at him, because that could definitely spell trouble for her career. No matter how close she and Hal were, their relationship would never withstand the slew of obscenities going through her mind. She ignored his remark about her being difficult to work with, well aware that more than a few people had that opinion of her, but she got the job done. And in the end, wasn't that what mattered?

"You're sure?" Hal sounded skeptical. "All parties involved are okay?"

"I'm sure," she said again, her tone clipped. She picked her keys up from the coffee table in front of her and hurled them across the room. That helped some, but the anger still seethed right underneath her calm façade. "We're heading back up there this afternoon."

"Good. I don't want to have to babysit any bruised egos."

"Not necessary, Hal. If she says it was a simple misunderstanding, then we'll find a way to work through it."

"All right," Hal said, seemingly satisfied with her response. "Now catch this guy before he kills another kid. I'm not at all happy with the number ending up dead lately."

"You and me both, Hal." She ended the call and somehow managed to stop herself just before she sent the phone to join her keys. "Fuck."

❖

The ride back to Walton Creek was tense, and Liv hadn't said more than two words to Sophie since she'd picked her up. About halfway to their destination, Sophie couldn't take the silence any longer.

"I'm sorry," she finally said, knowing her frustration was evident, and in turn, her apology sounded insincere. It really didn't matter if her request for forgiveness didn't appear genuine though. She stared out the window, refusing to look at Liv.

"For what?"

Was she serious? Sophie turned in her seat but didn't say anything.

Liv finally sighed. "Are you sorry for what happened last night, or for making sure you got in touch with Hal this morning before I did?"

"I'm not sorry about either one explicitly." Sophie didn't give her answer much thought. How dare Liv blame her exclusively for what happened last night? "I'm just sorry about all the tension between us."

Liv didn't say anything, but simply clenched her jaw. Sophie held on to the door handle when Liv suddenly swerved to take the exit for the service plaza off the turnpike.

"We need to get a couple of things straight right now," Liv said after she parked and turned off the ignition. "First, you don't *ever* go over my head to talk to my superior again. If you have a problem with me, then you talk to me about it. Second, what happened last night will never happen again. I made that mistake once, and I will *not* get trapped again."

Emotions flashed through Liv's eyes as she appeared stunned she'd actually spoken the words out loud. The pain that shrouded her eyes just before she looked away made Sophie want to touch her, but that would be wrong. She would do anything to take Liv's pain away, though she shouldn't be feeling that way.

"Talk to me, Liv," she said softly. "Somebody obviously hurt you pretty badly. Maybe it would help to tell me about it."

Liv shook her head but looked at Sophie for a moment, her expression inscrutable. When Liv stared out the windshield as she reached for the key, Sophie took a chance and placed her hand on Liv's forearm.

"Please," she said.

Liv closed her eyes, resting her head against the seat. "There was a woman I worked with a few years ago. She insisted she was straight, but that never stopped her from flirting with me." Liv turned her head to look out her side window and Sophie slowly pulled her hand away.

She continued to talk as though she didn't notice. "One night we went out with some other people to celebrate closing a big case. We had too much to drink, and she wouldn't stop touching me. She assured me she knew what she was doing and convinced me to go home with her. We ended up having an affair that lasted a few months, but when I decided to end it, she started screaming sexual harassment. I was her direct superior. She went to Hal trying to get me fired, but he knew me too well to believe the things she was saying. I've known him since the day I joined the Bureau. If anyone other than Hal had been my boss, my career would have been ruined. He somehow managed to keep it quiet, and she was assigned to a field office on the West Coast."

"It sucks you had to go through that, Liv, and I'm glad you trust me enough to tell me," Sophie said after a few moments of silence. "But I'm not trying to trap you."

"It was nice to be involved with someone who didn't hold the job against me," Liv said, sounding wistful.

Did Liv even realize she'd spoken the words aloud? Sophie's heart broke a little at the pain in Liv's voice, and in that moment of trust between them, she hoped they could at least be friends.

"I know what that's like," she said quietly, afraid she would break the spell between them if she spoke louder.

"Excuse me?" Liv turned in her seat to look at her. "You know what what's like?"

"Trying to find a woman who won't hold the job responsible for all the problems in a relationship." Sophie answered carefully. "I can't tell you how many times I've had a woman break up with me because she thought the job was more important to me than she was."

Liv stared at her in silence for a few minutes, and she forced herself not to look away, even though Liv's scrutiny made her uncomfortable. She felt Liv was evaluating her sincerity, and she didn't want to give Liv a reason to close herself off again. After what seemed an eternity, a ghost of a smile formed on Liv's lips.

"Apparently we have more in common that I thought, Kane." Liv's body visibly relaxed and she let the back of her head rest against the seat while she stared at the ceiling. "But things will not go any further between us than they did last night. I can't lose focus on this case. Besides that, getting involved with another team member is never a good idea."

"So if we weren't working on the same team..." When Liv looked at her Sophie put on her most innocent smile. At least she hoped that was how it looked.

"I'm not going to answer that, Kane." Liv straightened in her seat and turned the key.

"Well, then, I'm just going to put this out there, and you can do what you see fit with the information." Sophie took a deep breath. "In case you hadn't noticed, I'm attracted to you, Agent Andrews. I'm fairly sure I'm mature enough to be able to control my actions and simply be a friend and a colleague, but should you ever wonder if an advance would be welcome, I can assure you it most certainly would be."

Sophie smiled in satisfaction at the way Liv refused to look in her direction. They rode the rest of the way to Walton Creek in silence.

CHAPTER FIFTEEN

It had been almost a month since Mark had taken the boy. The kid definitely had anger issues, and he wasn't stupid enough to try to pass him off as healthy. Too much was at stake. Besides, he'd gotten new orders to get a girl. He had the perfect one in mind and had been planning her abduction for almost two weeks.

He pulled out his cell phone and called a number he'd committed to memory over the past few months, even though it was programmed into the phone. He paced back and forth outside the door to the basement while it rang.

"Yeah," the voice on the other end said just when Mark thought it would switch to voice mail.

"I need to kill the kid."

"And that's my problem why?" the man asked. "I told you to do it the day after you took him, for God's sake. Jesus, you're a fuckup, Marcus. I want that kid taken care of today, do you understand me? Dump the body in Forks Township, near the airport on Sullivan Trail. That's far enough away from where I am."

"Yes, sir," Mark said quietly as he rubbed his forehead.

"And another thing—the girl you take better not disappear from anywhere near Walton Creek, because I don't need this shit playing out in my own backyard. It's not my job to coordinate where you abduct and dump bodies. You really shouldn't have to dump any bodies though, should you, Marcus? You are seriously trying my patience. I should kill you and your mother now and cut my losses before you fuck anything else up."

"I need to talk to my cousin this morning at the diner in Walton Creek, but he's being followed. Can you do something about it?" Mark worried there would be another outburst and tried to change the subject. He wasn't disappointed.

"Jesus, Kraft, I regret the day I ever got you involved in this. You've been nothing but a screwup since day one." After a pause, Mark thought they'd been disconnected. "You get one more chance, you understand? One more mistake, and I swear to you it will be your last. I'll take care of the tail on your cousin, but I want the girl in the next two days."

The call went dead and Mark began to pace again, trying to work up the nerve to do what he needed to do to Timmy York.

He thought he'd steeled himself with the Henderson girl and the boy before that, but nothing could ever prepare him for the amount of blood. He couldn't use a gun, because that would make too much noise. He sure didn't want to call attention to what he was doing. A knife was the only way, but it felt so much more personal. It wasn't personal for him though—he had nothing against these kids. And God, how could a small child have that much blood in its body?

He pulled the hunting knife out of its sheath behind his back and looked at it for a moment. His heart sped up when he thought about what he was about to do with it. He felt sick and tried to still his shaking hands, but nothing worked. He took a deep breath and opened the door.

"Hey, Timmy," he called out, his voice shaking. "We're going to go for a ride. I'm going to take you home now, all right?"

Three weeks after the ball game all hell broke loose in Walton Creek. Liv had somehow managed to work the schedule so she and Sophie were never alone in their hotel room together, but they were getting closer with each passing day. She would touch Sophie's arm or place a hand on her shoulder as they spoke about the case, but couldn't help herself. It was almost as though she needed the connection with Sophie, and the thought scared her. She'd never *needed* anyone before. Wanted, yes, but never needed. Neither of them had mentioned what happened the night of the ball game, or the conversation that had taken place on the ride back to Walton Creek from Philadelphia. Liv wasn't sure how much longer she could deny her growing attraction, and she wasn't sure she even wanted to. It took so much more energy to ignore it than to simply give in.

She walked into the command center to relieve the overnight shift and was surprised to see only Justin there.

"Where's Victor?" she asked as she took a seat and began to go over the notes they'd made.

"He went to get coffee and some sandwiches," Justin answered, his attention riveted to the computer screen in front of him.

"Why? You guys are going off shift now." When Justin didn't respond, Liv suddenly had a sinking feeling. "Justin, when did he leave?"

"About twenty minutes ago, I think."

"The time, Ingram," she said, her impatience growing.

"Around five," he answered. Liv observed him in silence as he looked at his watch and it suddenly dawned on him. "Oh, shit."

"That was two hours ago." She pulled out her phone and called Victor's cell, but didn't get an answer. After she called the other team members and ordered everyone on duty until further notice, she finally spared Justin a glance. "What the hell are you doing that has you so wrapped up over there?"

"Frank started searching for other kidnappings in the area to see if we could figure out where he might strike next," he said. He had his cell phone out and Liv assumed he was continuously trying to call Victor as he spoke. "I was trying to figure it all out. There's a pattern but I'm just not seeing it."

"Did he go to the diner?"

"Yeah, that's where we've been getting food."

Liv could see the genuine concern on his face each time Victor's voice mail came on. "Liv, I'm sorry. I really didn't know he'd been gone so long."

"I'm going over there to see if anybody can tell me what happened. Send Kane over when she gets here." She wanted to tell him it was okay, that it wasn't his fault. But she couldn't, because if something happened to Victor Nathan, it might have been avoided if Justin had been paying attention to the time.

"Will do, Boss," Justin said, hitting redial.

❖

"Nobody saw anything?" Sophie asked as she paced.

Her irritation was evident, and Liv had to look away from her. Even frustrated she was sexy as hell. Her mind didn't need to be going there right now.

"He's not a small man, Liv. How could no one have seen him leave here?"

"He was here at five in the morning. I'm just guessing, but Walton Creek doesn't seem like the kind of town that wakes up that early." Liv stood next to Justin's car, which Victor had driven to the diner to get their food and coffee. Unfortunately he'd parked it near the rear of the building where there weren't any windows. Maybe if he'd parked closer to the front door someone might have seen something. The waitress confirmed Victor had gone in and picked up their order, but had come and gone on his own. They weren't that far from Allentown, but they were far enough off the major roads that the diner didn't get much drive-by traffic. More often than not, if they had customers, they were people who knew the diner was there.

"But where could he be? Why would he have left Justin's car here?"

"Let me know if you come up with any answers, Kane," Liv said, her own feelings threatening to take over. "I've been trying to figure it out since I got here. He's not the type to get in a vehicle with someone he doesn't know, even if he was having car trouble. Hell, the motel is only half a mile from here. He would have called Justin if there was a problem."

"Any word?" Justin asked as he got out of Frank's car. Since Frank was with him, that left only Gabe at the station.

"No, nothing." Liv watched in silence as Justin got in his own car and tried to start it with his spare key. Nothing happened. She motioned for him to pop the hood. As soon as she got it up, she saw the battery had been disconnected, and two of the spark plugs were missing. No way in hell had the car arrived at the diner like that, which could only mean someone had deliberately sabotaged it. But why? Her cell phone rang and she took a few steps away to answer it. "Andrews."

"Agent Andrews, this is Sergeant Mansfield. We've found Agent Nathan."

"Where is he?" Liv could tell by his voice she wouldn't like the answer. He didn't sound like the normally cocky asshole she'd come to know.

"Dead," he answered, "behind the motel. The night manager came across the body when she was taking out some office trash and called it in."

"We'll be right there." Liv disconnected the call and turned to her team, all of whom had been listening to what little there'd been on her end of the conversation. "Franklin, you and Kane head back to the station and wait there for my call. Justin, you're coming with me."

"Where is he?" Sophie asked.

Liv didn't like the worry on Sophie's face—on everyone's face—so before she got into her SUV, she simply said, "He's dead. I'll call when I have more to report."

"Fuck, Liv," Justin said when they pulled out of the parking lot and headed for the motel. "Why would somebody kill him?"

"I don't know." Liv answered with no emotion. "Maybe he stumbled on a drug deal? Maybe somebody just doesn't like federal agents? We don't even know if he was murdered, Ingram." She paused for a moment, and a thought sprang to the front of her mind. "Maybe he tried to stop a kidnapping."

"And he had to be shut up?" Justin asked skeptically. "That makes no sense. Everybody around here knows we're in town, and we go to the diner several times a day. Why would the prick nab a kid from there?"

"I don't know the reasons, Ingram," Liv said, her tone more brusque than she intended. She took a deep breath to try to calm her nerves as she pulled into the motel parking lot. She shut off the engine and turned in her seat to face Justin. "I'm sorry. I don't understand it any more than you do. We just have to assume at this point that his death is related to the case we're working. Hell, maybe he had a heart attack or something, and it isn't as sinister as we're thinking it is. I hung up on Officer Friendly before he could give me much information."

"It's all my fault." Justin looked like he was about to cry. Liv tried to ignore the panic she felt at the prospect.

"Listen to me, you can't think like that, Justin. We have to look at it as a deliberate and calculated move. If you'd been with him, or even gone out to look for him when he didn't come right back, I could be dealing with two dead team members. Tell me now if you aren't going to be able to deal with it. I'll call Gabe to come take your place."

"I'm fine, Boss," he said after a moment. He wiped his eyes and looked at her earnestly. "Let's do this."

They got out of the car and walked to the back of the building. Mansfield, wearing street clothes, stood next to an officer she recognized but had only met in passing at the station. She glanced at Mansfield again. It was coming up on eight in the morning, and he should have been working so he should have been in uniform. She walked to the body and crouched down next to it, immediately noting the single gunshot wound to Victor's temple, his FBI-issued Glock held loosely in his right hand. Suicide? Liv seriously doubted it, even if at first glance it seemed to be. None of her team members were the type to take their own life.

"Why didn't anyone hear a gunshot?" Liv asked.

"The closest house is a good mile from here," Mansfield told her. "It doesn't surprise me nobody heard it."

"Someone had to be working in the motel," Justin said from behind Liv. "I know we're on the other side of the building, but the office is only about a hundred feet away. They had to have heard something, right?"

"Has anyone talked to them yet?" Liv asked, still studying the bullet hole and the way Victor Nathan was lying on the ground. It didn't add up, and she didn't wait for a response. "Justin, go get my camera and then talk to the people working here."

"I'm sorry, ma'am, but I didn't think I needed to. It looks like a suicide to me," the uniformed officer said.

Liv stood and backed up a few paces so she was standing between the two men. She motioned toward the body as she looked at Mansfield, wanting to gauge his reaction.

"You don't think it looks odd?" she asked.

"How so?"

"It appears to me he was on his knees." She walked back over to Victor in order to show Mansfield what she was talking about. The other officer was kneeling down to look at the indentations in the dirt, but when she turned back to Mansfield, he was still in the same spot, looking a bit green. "Don't tell me this is the first body you've had to deal with."

He muttered something under his breath as he stood next to her. Liv studied him for a moment, wondering why he was refusing to look her in the eye. She chalked it up to him not liking the fact she was taking over. But Victor Nathan was a federal agent, damn it. After the way Mansfield had screwed up in the first few hours of the York kidnapping, she sure as hell wouldn't trust him to investigate the death of one of her people.

"Look at the way his legs are bent. And the ground's a little soft, so you can still see where his knees made an impression in the dirt." She paused long enough to take the camera from Justin and to think for a split second how Mansfield made her feel like she was training a rookie. "Someone definitely wanted us to believe it was a suicide, but they didn't take the time to make sure everything was set up just right."

"Why would somebody kill him?" Mansfield asked, his hands shaking as he shoved them in his pockets.

"You're missing a button on your shirt, Sergeant," Liv said absently as she knelt back down to look at Victor, noticing Mansfield's stomach poking through the gap in his shirt. She didn't want to talk to him about anything. He seemed like he was an intruder on a family tragedy, and she wanted him as far away from it as possible. She closed her eyes to calm herself and silently gave thanks for her ability to shut off all emotions. When she opened them again, she felt a tear slide down her cheek and swiped at it. She slid Victor's eyes closed and vowed she would find who killed him. After angrily wiping another tear away, she stood and turned back to face Mansfield.

"Why aren't you in uniform, Sergeant?" she asked.

"I was tailing Richard Kraft when the call came over the radio about a body being found here." Mansfield paced around the scene, presumably looking for any other signs that someone else had been at the scene. "Kraft was on his way to work, and since I was driving right by the motel I decided to do a quick pass around it."

"Then who's tailing him now?"

"Huh?" He grunted, finally looking at her.

"I asked who you have tailing Kraft now. Why would you leave a suspect you're supposed to be watching?"

"Like I said, he was on his way to work," Mansfield said defensively. "Do you have any idea how boring it is to sit outside that school all fucking day while he's teaching? Trust me, he isn't going anywhere until the school day's over."

"I don't give a rat's ass how exciting or boring your job is," Liv said, giving rein to her anger. "You had one assignment, and now he could be out there abducting another child."

"He hasn't done anything out of the ordinary in all the time we've been watching him."

"If another kid turns up missing, it's going to cost you your job, Mansfield. Do you understand what I'm telling you?" Livid, she didn't care she was taking out her rage on him. "Get over there now, and I better not hear he was late for work this morning."

"I'll send Parsons," he said, and Liv didn't have the strength to argue with him. She knelt again and began taking pictures of the scene. A scene from a nightmare.

CHAPTER SIXTEEN

It was well past two in the afternoon when Liv pulled into the parking lot at the police station, talking to Hal on the Bluetooth. She had nothing against the coroner's office in Allentown, but Hal wanted their own people to handle things, so Victor's body was on its way back to Philadelphia for an autopsy. Liv had forwarded all the photos she'd taken to Hal before she'd left the scene.

"I agree with you, Andrews, it doesn't look like a suicide based on the pictures," he said as she turned off the ignition. "We'll have to wait for the autopsy report, but if he didn't pull the trigger himself, we'll know based on trajectory and gunshot residue."

"Hal, I don't care if he did pull the trigger," Liv said. She was running on autopilot and knew the grief at losing a member of her team would hit her at some point. She couldn't let it be now though, because she had to find Victor's murderer. "The car being disabled is enough to tell me we're dealing with a homicide. He saw something, and he was killed because of it."

"I know, Liv," he said, his tone indicating he was fighting back emotions of his own. "We'll get to the bottom of it."

"You'll call me as soon as you hear anything?"

"You know I will. Have you had any more problems with Kane?"

"No, it was a misunderstanding, just like she said." She glanced at her reflection in the rearview mirror, struck by how tired she looked. These last two cases had taken a toll on her, and now she had a dead agent. When would life go her way for once? Could the day get any worse than it already was?

She was walking into their command center when she saw Sophie standing by the sink, with Beth Parsons standing next to her—a little too close for Liv's liking. Liv felt a flash of what could only be called jealousy when she saw Sophie laugh and Officer Parsons place a hand low on Sophie's back. Liv cleared her throat loudly and took some degree of pleasure in the way Parsons pulled her hand away like she'd been burned.

Sophie's eyes met hers, and Liv, her adrenaline apparently running out, almost collapsed at her worried look. Luckily a chair sat next to her so she covered herself.

"Are you all right, Liv?" Sophie asked tentatively.

"No, I'm not. I just shipped off the corpse of one of my agents for an autopsy. How's your day going?" Liv couldn't keep the sarcasm out of her voice and didn't want to. She turned her attention to the officer next to Sophie. "Parsons, I thought you were tailing Kraft. What the hell are you doing here flirting with Kane?"

"What? Nobody told me that," Parsons said as she glanced at Sophie. Liv watched the interaction between them with more interest than she wanted to have. Sophie didn't appear as comfortable with the officer as Parsons evidently wanted her to be.

"Where the fuck is Sergeant Dickhead?" Liv stood and registered the surprise on Sophie's face before snapping her attention back to Parsons. How dare that jackass undermine her authority? She walked to Parsons but stopped when she noticed the other woman trying to back away from her. She lowered her voice, but instead of a reassuring tone, her words came out as a menacing growl. "Where is he?"

"I don't know, ma'am," Parsons said, shaking her head and looking like a trapped animal.

"I'm going to fry his ass," Liv murmured before turning to head for his office.

"He's not here," Parsons told her. When Liv turned back around, she saw Parsons looking to Sophie for help, but Sophie was obviously as surprised as Liv was. "He took the afternoon off."

"Well, isn't that just peachy?" It took all the effort she could muster to not punch a hole through the wall. She began to pace in front of the table where Justin was monitoring the computer equipment, apparently trying to stay out of her way. She turned her wrath on him. "Did you know about this, Ingram?"

"No, Boss," he answered with a shake of his head. "It's the first I've heard of it. I assumed you sent Mansfield back out to tail Kraft."

"I want his home address now, Parsons," she said, pulling out her ever-present bottle of aspirin and swallowing two pills. She sat in the chair next to Justin and rested her head on her arms, which she folded on the table in front of her.

"What about dinner tonight, Sophie?" Parsons asked quietly. Liv stood once again, causing the chair to topple over behind her, and turned to face the young officer.

"I'm sorry, but what about my statement led you to believe I have all day for you to get me the information I requested, Officer?" Liv took great joy in the fear in Parsons's eyes as the woman scurried around her and out of the room. When she was gone, Liv turned to Sophie. "Flirting with her is not appropriate, Kane. We talked about that before. Do I really need to point it out to you again?"

"I wasn't flirting." Sophie took a step forward, obviously not about to back down. "She asked me to dinner and I turned her down, Liv. No need to get so angry."

Sophie placed a hand on Liv's arm, and she wanted to pull away. She wanted that more than anything, but Sophie's touch grounded her. She hated that she couldn't shut down her emotions with Sophie the way she'd always been able to with women. Something about Sophie was working methodically to erode the walls she'd erected around her heart, and it was unnerving. She glanced around the room and saw Justin watching their interaction with a slight grin. That jerked her back squarely into the reality of what was happening. She pulled away quickly and turned toward the door.

"I need to get some air." Parsons hadn't come back with Mansfield's address yet, but Liv had to get away. Jealousy was so not her thing, and she was having trouble dealing with it on top of everything else. Justin was smart enough to send someone to pick Sergeant Dickhead up without her giving explicit instructions. She walked past her vehicle without so much as a glance and kept right on walking out of the parking lot.

With Victor's death it might not be the smartest thing to do, going off on her own, but given the way she felt at the moment, she'd rip the guy's throat out if he tried to come after her. Part of her really hoped he'd try.

She'd been walking for twenty minutes when she registered the sound of her cell phone ringing. She slowed her gait and reached for the phone on her hip.

"Andrews," she said curtly.

"Liv, it's Justin. We just got a call from someone who says they saw Timmy York."

"Alive?" Liv stopped walking and sat down on a rock about four feet off the road. Her pulse spiked at the thought of a new lead.

"Yeah. At a grocery store in Forks Township at the corner of Sullivan Trail and Uhler Road. Across the street from a small airport." Justin sounded as excited as Liv felt. "The local cops there are interviewing the woman, but I thought you'd probably want to be there as well."

"You know me pretty well, Justin." Finding bodies was not what Liv had in mind when she'd decided to apply for the CARD unit, and her adrenaline kicked in at the possibility they could save Timmy before he became another statistic. She wanted to find kids alive and be able to return them to distraught parents more than anything.

"Where are you?" Justin asked.

"I turned right out of the parking lot and I'm walking on the highway that goes by the station." She looked back down the road and saw a police car heading toward her, lights flashing and sirens blaring. "I see a cruiser coming my way now."

"That's Parsons. Flag her down," Justin said. "Sophie's already on her way to the scene."

❖

"I'm sorry if I was stepping on your toes earlier, ma'am," Parsons said when Liv was situated in the passenger seat.

"What?"

"With Agent Kane," she explained, speeding down the road. "I'm sorry if I was out of line."

"I am not having this conversation with you right now, Parsons." Liv knew she should just tell her there was nothing between her and Sophie, but she couldn't believe the audacity of this woman to bring the situation up while driving to the site of their first real break in the case. Besides, it would be fun to make her squirm a bit. "In fact, I don't want to talk with you right now. I've had a colossally bad day, so just shut up and drive."

"Yes, ma'am."

Liv stared out the passenger window at the farmhouses they passed and couldn't help but think about Sophie. As much as she wanted to deny it, her life seemed somehow brighter since Sophie showed up. Liv didn't understand it, but for the first time ever, she had real feelings for someone. Crazy, because she didn't even know Sophie that well, but she was sure of what she was experiencing. She spared a quick glance at the woman driving the cruiser.

It irritated her to realize Parsons's attention to Sophie could cause the jealousy she'd felt earlier. Sophie clearly didn't have any interest in Parsons, but it still irked Liv to see the way Parsons touched the small of Sophie's back as they talked. It seemed such an intimate gesture, and she didn't want anyone touching Sophie like that.

She wasn't at all sure she had the strength to fight her attraction to Sophie much longer. The physical attraction was certainly there, but the emotional pull to Sophie was even more unsettling. The overwhelming desire to have Sophie comfort her after Victor's death scared the hell out of her. She shook her head to try to dispel the images that made her decidedly uncomfortable.

"We'll be there in a couple more minutes, ma'am," Parsons said, pulling Liv out of her thoughts.

"I told you to stop calling me that," Liv said as she sat up straighter. "When we get there, you can head back to the station. Agent Kane will give me a ride back."

"Yes, ma'am," she said, glancing quickly toward Liv. Before Liv could say anything, she corrected herself. "I mean Agent Andrews."

"Tell me about Sergeant Mansfield, Parsons," Liv said when they pulled off the highway.

"What do you want to know?"

"Is he a prick to everyone he meets, or just the women?"

Liv watched as Parsons checked the rearview mirror more times than was necessary, obviously trying to avoid the question. Liv was about to give up when she finally answered.

"I think you'd be hard-pressed to find anyone in the department who likes the man."

"Why is that?"

"Well, you've seen how he treats women, and if you'll pardon the expression, he thinks his shit doesn't stink," Parsons said, obviously uncomfortable talking about her superior behind his back. "Long story short, he's an asshole."

Parsons pulled the cruiser alongside Liv's SUV, and Liv got out without a word. Sophie stood speaking to a uniformed officer and a civilian woman away from the front entrance of the grocery store. When Parsons pulled out of the parking lot she tried to ignore the relief that washed through her because she wouldn't have to watch Parsons paw at Sophie.

"What do we have?" she asked when Sophie looked at her. Liv flashed her badge to the others and took a quick look at Sophie's notes.

"This is Roberta Claiborne, the woman who saw Timmy."

"Hi, I'm Agent Andrews," Liv said, extending a hand in greeting. "I'm sure you've already been asked, but what can you tell us about the vehicle you saw?"

"It was a green pickup, newer model, Ford, I think."

"Do we have a license-plate number?" Liv asked the officer.

"No, ma'am," he answered with a shake of his head. "Just the last number on the plate."

"Well, that's better than nothing, and a hell of a lot more than we had before."

"I'm sorry I didn't see the plate, but the truck was coming toward me," she said. "He was driving too fast for me to be able to see it after he passed. But that little boy was sitting in the passenger seat looking out the window, and I know for sure it was the same little boy who's missing."

"That's just one reason I hate that this state doesn't require front plates." Liv smiled at Roberta Claiborne. "It's not your fault, ma'am. You've certainly given us enough to help us narrow down our search. Are you certain it was a Pennsylvania tag?"

"Definitely." The woman nodded. "And I'm sure it was that little boy."

"Good." Liv pulled out a business card for her. "If you think of anything else you haven't already mentioned, please don't hesitate to call, day or night."

"I will. And I hope you find the man and bring that little boy home. A lot of people around here are scared to death to let their kids out of their sight."

When she left, Liv turned to Sophie. "Call Justin and have him start running the plate information."

"I already did."

"Oh. Good," Liv said, pleasantly surprised. She turned to the Forks Township officer. "I'll need a copy of your report faxed to the Walton Creek Police Department."

"Yes, ma'am, Agent Kane already gave me the number. I'll have it to you in an hour or so."

Liv stood there speechless as he tipped his hat and walked back to his cruiser. After a moment she turned back to Sophie.

"I guess I didn't even need to come out here, did I?"

"Of course you did," Sophie said with a smile. "You're the team leader. You need to meet the witnesses and form your own conclusions. Besides, I have your vehicle."

"Good point." Liv allowed herself a smile. It felt good to be able to kid around with Sophie after the horror they'd dealt with that morning. It felt good to be able to finally have a lead in the abduction case, no matter how thin it might be. Timmy York wasn't dead yet, which meant they still had time. Why the kidnapper was driving around with him in full view was a mystery, but as long as Timmy was alive, she didn't care.

"Oh, crap," Sophie said, her smile fading quickly as she looked over Liv's shoulder.

Liv turned to see the Yorks hurrying across the parking lot toward them. Her confusion at seeing them must have been obvious because Sophie's hand closed around her wrist.

"How the hell could they know we have a lead?" Sophie asked quietly. "There's no way this could have hit the news yet."

Liv shrugged as she took a step toward them.

"Mr. and Mrs. York, what are you doing here?"

"We heard you found Timmy," Peter said, looking frantically between the two of them.

"Where did you hear that?" Sophie asked, stepping forward to stand next to Liv.

"We got a phone call," Abby replied, clearly scanning the area for her son. "Where is he?"

Liv could see she'd been crying and looked away. Sophie took Abby York by the arm and led her to one side. Liv breathed a sigh of relief.

"Is it true? Did you find his…" Peter choked back a sob and looked across the street at the small airfield. He took a deep breath and turned his attention back to Liv. "Did you find his body?"

"What?" Liv asked, trying not to notice the tear running down his cheek. The only thing that made her more uncomfortable than a crying woman was a crying man. "Who called you?"

"I don't know. He wouldn't give his name. He just said you'd found Timmy at the airport here," he said, gesturing across the street.

Liv's heart plummeted. She looked across the street as she dialed Justin's cell phone. She looked back to Peter and shook her head.

"No, we haven't found his body," she said as she listened to the phone ringing in her ear. "We had a witness who saw him alive, and that's why we're here."

"Oh, thank God."

"Ingram," Justin said, and Liv walked away when Mr. York moved to join his wife and Sophie.

"Justin, I need people at Braden Airport in Forks Township now. I don't care if you send Walton Creek or if you send Forks, but I need them here now."

"Sure thing," he said before she heard him telling Frank to get people out there. "What's going on, Liv?"

"Somebody made an anonymous call to the Yorks to tell them we'd found their son's body at the airfield. Hold on a second," she said before walking back to Peter. "Do you have anything of Timmy's with you?"

"There's a baseball hat in the car."

"Get it for me," she said. When he turned to run back to the vehicle, Liv resumed her phone conversation. "Make sure we have a tracking dog too. I doubt he's there, but we need to cover our bases. The witness here said he was in a green pickup, just like the witness said the day he was abducted. He was alive when she saw him, and I can't imagine the bastard would have killed him and dumped the body here with police present."

"I'll take care of it now. Anything else?"

"You have any interesting hits on the partial plate yet?"

"Negative, but I'm still working on it."

"Call me if anything comes up." Liv ended the call as Peter York returned with the hat. She took it and told him to stay put. "We're going to search the airfield, but I need you and your wife to stay out of the way, understood?"

The last thing she needed was to have the distraught parents impede their search. She knew better than to suggest they go home and wait, because she sure as hell wouldn't if she were in their position.

CHAPTER SEVENTEEN

L iv dropped into the chair at the desk in their hotel room and rested her head on her folded arms. The search of the airfield had been slow, and ultimately unnecessary. The dog hadn't picked up Timmy's scent anywhere, but she still ordered a thorough search of the entire field, including the lone house next to it.

"Why would someone call the Yorks and tell them we found a body?" Sophie asked.

Liv watched her pull clothes out of her suitcase before she headed to the shower. She looked away when a lacy bra landed on top of the pile.

"I've been trying to figure that out all day, Sophie. Maybe they were trying to keep us busy."

"But why?"

"So he could kill him and dump the body somewhere else? I really don't know." She sat straighter in her chair as Sophie walked to the bathroom. "I felt optimistic for about five minutes this afternoon. Now I'm feeling nothing but dread."

"I know. For the kidnapper to have had Timmy in a relatively isolated area can't be good." Sophie gently touched Liv's arm on her way into the bathroom. "Don't wait up for me. You need to sleep."

She nodded as the bathroom door shut and then she was alone with her thoughts. She stretched out on her bed, fully clothed, and closed her eyes. Her phone vibrated on her hip and she groaned, forcing her eyes back open to glance at the screen.

"Hal," she said, suddenly feeling the weight of everything she'd dealt with since she'd woken up that morning. "You have preliminary results on Victor, I hope?"

"Definitely a homicide, Liv. No gunshot residue on his hands, so he didn't pull the trigger himself. The trajectory of the bullet indicates the killer was standing above him, shooting downward." Hal sounded even more tired than she felt, if that was possible.

"Fuck." Liv swallowed back the bile in her throat. She'd sensed it hadn't been a suicide, but having her instincts confirmed didn't make her feel any better. And it sure as hell didn't bring Victor back.

"I spoke with his wife this afternoon."

"I hate to ask, but how is she?"

"She's taking the kids and going to stay with her folks in New York for a bit. It really pisses me off that someone killed one of my agents, Andrews. Have you found any leads on either Victor's murder or the abduction?"

"We're running some information through the database as we speak. Hopefully by this time tomorrow we'll have something concrete. A witness saw Timmy York, alive, at a small airport north of here. We're following up."

"Good," he said with a sigh that spoke volumes about his mood. "Keep me updated."

"I always do."

Sophie emerged from the bathroom, hair wet, and wearing sweatpants and a tank top. She pointed at the phone Liv held in her hands. "When's the last time you slept?"

"I don't know," Liv said with a sigh. Her mouth went dry at the sight of Sophie fresh from the shower, her tank top clinging to her beautiful body. She looked at her phone before setting it on the bedside table. "Hal just called. Victor didn't commit suicide."

"You aren't surprised, are you?"

"No."

"You think his murder and the kidnappings are connected?"

"Yes. Victor was killed to keep us occupied or because he saw something he shouldn't have. It's all a little too coincidental."

"Then it has to be someone who knows who we are, because Justin's Toyota doesn't exactly scream FBI. They were waiting for him."

"It could have been any one of us." She didn't want to lead Sophie down any one path so she didn't say anything to indicate where her thoughts were. "Victor was just in the wrong place at the wrong time. It wouldn't make any sense for our perp to draw attention to himself by killing a federal agent. Victor had to have stumbled onto something."

"It was rather odd Mansfield was there at the scene, isn't it?" Sophie focused her attention to Liv's face, and Liv nodded. "He was bored trailing Kraft so he veered off to check on the call about a dead body?"

"I wondered that same thing this morning. His story was plausible though. The school where Kraft works really isn't very far from the motel, and he would have driven right past it."

"Why was he the one tailing Kraft in the first place? I get the impression he thinks he's too good for menial work like that. Why wouldn't he have delegated the surveillance to someone else?"

Liv felt her heart speed up as she realized they were on the same wavelength. It was always exhilarating to know you weren't the only one having doubts about someone. Usually she had these conversations with Justin, but it was equally invigorating to be talking things through with Sophie.

"You don't think Mansfield could have murdered Victor, do you?" Sophie asked after a few moments.

"I don't want to think it, but how can I not?" Liv ran a hand through her hair and sighed. "He's there with Victor's body when Justin and I arrive, and then while we're all busy with a suicide that turns out to be a homicide—and no one's watching Kraft—Timmy York is seen alive and someone calls his parents saying his body was found at virtually the same location. What are we missing? And where the hell is Mansfield now? He disappeared right in the middle of everything today after ignoring my explicit instructions to put a tail on Kraft again. It's too convenient."

"I understand what you're saying, and yes, the man's an ass, but that doesn't make him guilty of a crime, does it? What would be the motive?"

"Unless he's involved in the kidnappings, I can't see a motive for murdering a federal agent," Liv said tiredly.

"I'm having a hard time believing he could be involved."

"There are bad cops everywhere, Sophie, not just in the big cities like New York and Philadelphia."

"I know, but again, what's the motive?" Sophie asked.

Liv's eyes narrowed and Sophie felt as though she was watching something play out no one else could see, something she couldn't follow because Liv had virtually shut her out since their return from Philadelphia. If only Liv would talk to her and hadn't been going to such great lengths to not be alone with her for the past few weeks. But she didn't know how to change the situation between them. "Let's not discuss this anymore tonight, all right? We both need to rest."

"You're right. Get some sleep."

"Liv?" Sophie asked after a few moments. She waited for Liv to look at her before going on. "Tell me about your birth parents. What happened to them?"

"What?" Liv looked at her, obviously surprised.

Sophie regretted the question immediately. "I'm sorry. It's none of my business."

"My mother died of a drug overdose," Liv said without emotion.

How could she sound so detached? Sophie silently watched her pull a pair of shorts and a T-shirt from her suitcase to sleep in. "She had enough heroin in her system to kill two adult horses. The police knew she didn't inject herself, because she couldn't have been alive to finish it. My father was convicted of murdering her and is currently serving a life sentence in New York State."

"Have you ever seen him?" Sophie shrank when Liv leveled her with an icy stare. She'd never seen so much anger reflected in someone's eyes.

"I was eight months old when she was murdered. She'd run away from home and no one knew how to find her family. *His* family blamed her for all of his problems and saw me as the spawn of the devil. They refused to have anything to do with me, which is why I ended up in the foster system. He took her away from me. I've never met him, and I have no desire to ever see him."

Sophie was silent as Liv disappeared into the bathroom, slamming the door behind her. She regretted dredging up the past, because it obviously pained Liv to talk about it, but she couldn't help feeling a bit honored. As private as Liv was, she probably hadn't shared that story with many people in her life.

She wanted to be asleep when Liv came out of the bathroom, but by the time she turned onto her side and closed her eyes, she was back. She pretended to be asleep so Liv wouldn't feel like she had to talk to her anymore.

Liv knew Sophie wasn't asleep but was grateful for the reprieve. She slid under the covers and her mind went immediately to the case. She wished to God she could take a magic pill that would allow her to see the kidnapper and murderer, but none existed. And it infuriated her more than she would ever let on that their perp was managing to stay a step ahead of them. But what could she do? She turned away from Sophie and closed her eyes, willing sleep to claim her, but she'd be lucky to rest at all. She tried to steady her breathing, relieved when Sophie's breathing finally indicated she was asleep.

She turned onto her back and stared up at the ceiling, watching the reflection of the occasional headlight of a car driving by. She couldn't believe she'd told Sophie about her parents. Cindy, Justin, and the Andrewses were the only people in her life who knew that about her past, and she hated that it still bothered her. Because both of her biological parents had been drug addicts, a life with them would have been hell, but a part of her always wondered about a life that might have been. She loved Janet and Kyle Andrews and in them had found the unconditional love and support every child needs in a parent. She shook her head to dispel the thoughts of her biological parents, because they made her feel she was somehow being unfaithful to the Andrewses.

She kept thinking about Sophie, picturing her wet and soft from the shower. That was a dangerous road to go down. Liv had almost taken her in her arms and kissed her. The thought shook her, and she turned onto her side facing away from Sophie before punching her pillow and closing her eyes again.

She focused on her anger at Mansfield and forced herself to think about the things she'd say to him the next morning. A smile tugged at her lips, and she finally fell asleep with the vision of the overweight sergeant hanging by his toes.

Mark was wide-awake. He knew he was in deep trouble the second he'd decided not to kill Timmy. He just couldn't do it. He also couldn't go back to the house because Mark knew *he* would come looking for him.

He glanced at Timmy sleeping on the other bed in the motel room. Timmy had been excited when Mark told him he was taking him home. He hated lying to the kid, but he had to in order to keep him happy. When he'd gotten to the airport, the boy had started crying, and Mark knew he couldn't do it again. He gave Timmy a candy bar and told him they had to wait a little while, but everything would be okay. The kid had kicked the dash until it dented, but eventually he'd calmed down and eaten the candy bar before falling asleep. Mark stared at him. What the hell was he going to do with him?

Mark had called his mother to tell her she needed to go away for a few days, and even though she had begged him to tell her why, he'd just kept insisting she go to her sister's place out of state. He thought she believed him, but he couldn't be sure.

He'd make the other phone call in the morning, to try to explain why he hadn't killed Timmy. He hoped he could buy himself some more time by assuring the man on the other end of the line he'd have the girl he'd been ordered to find by the next night.

He stretched out on his own bed and closed his eyes, but sleep wouldn't claim him. He had the horrible feeling he'd never be able to sleep again.

CHAPTER EIGHTEEN

L iv strode into the police station the next morning like a woman on a mission. She barely registered the uniformed officers scrambling to get out of her way as she walked straight through the reception area and didn't stop until she'd reached Mansfield's office door. She hesitated for only a second—just long enough to take a deep, settling breath—before throwing the door open.

"The sooner the better—" he was saying into the telephone. He jumped back when the door crashed against the wall. "I'll call you later. Make sure you're around."

"We need to talk, Mansfield."

"What the fuck gives you the right to barge into my office?" He jumped out of his chair as he hung up the phone, but when Liv slammed the door shut and stalked around the desk to face him, he shrank back quickly.

"No, Mansfield, you don't get to be pissed off at me, and I don't have to answer any of your questions. You, however, will most definitely be answering mine. What gives you the right to circumvent my orders?" she asked, not even trying to keep her voice down. The outer-office area was silent, and she knew everyone was trying to listen in. Her people included. "You should not have pulled surveillance off Kraft without my approval."

"But we got a report the York kid was seen in Forks. It couldn't have been Kraft because he was at work when the sighting happened, and he doesn't own a green pickup." Mansfield sounded like a scared kid, and Liv glanced at the floor, half expecting to see a wet spot spreading around his feet. "Since we've been tailing him we've only ever seen him driving the Jeep, and his wife drives a Honda."

"That isn't really the point though, is it, Sergeant?" Liv took a step back, fighting the urge to grab him by the throat. She desperately wanted to tell him her suspicions regarding his behavior the day before, but with no real evidence against him, she couldn't let him know she considered him a suspect. Having him turn tail and run now would make things more difficult for her investigation. And if he really was just a dumb-ass, accusing him wouldn't do any good. "This is a federal investigation, and you are working for *me*. I had my people running computer searches and out in the field talking to whoever might have seen *anything* out of place, and all I asked you to do was keep an eye on Kraft. How would you feel if you gave a direct order to someone working for you, and they decided that your order was pointless so they wouldn't carry it out? What would you do to that officer, Sergeant?"

"Charge him with insubordination," he said without hesitation. Liv knew her smile wasn't a pleasant sight. She went to the door and opened it so everyone wouldn't have to strain to hear what she was about to say.

"And that's exactly what I did, Sergeant. I set it in motion first thing this morning. You should be getting a call relieving you of your duties any time now. I really wish I could say it was a pleasure working with you, but my mother taught me never to lie. And don't go anywhere because since you were first on the scene in Agent Nathan's death, we'll probably have some questions for you."

Liv slammed the door again before heading to the conference room where Justin had taken over the computers while Frank got a few hours' sleep. He looked up at her when she sat down, not bothering to hide his smirk.

"Remind me never to cross you," he said. A chime sounded from the computer and he turned his attention back to it. Liv watched his eyes grow wide while he read what was there.

"What is it?"

"Holy shit," he muttered. "I just got an e-mail from Gabe. He's out checking on one of the hits we got on a green Ford pickup. The license plate matches, and the guy showed him a bill of sale from two months ago. He sold it to a Marcus Kraft."

"Did he give a reason for not notifying the authorities of the sale?"

"He and the one he sold it to have prison records," Jason said. "Not surprising that the paperwork never got done on it."

"Maybe Richard has a brother?" Liv asked as she pulled her cell phone out and began to dial. She hoped it was something that simple and they wouldn't find out Marcus was his middle name. "That could explain why Mrs. Cunningham thought it was him on the footage they showed on television. Give me the address."

"Won't do any good." Justin slammed his fist on the table. "Gabe already ran it. The guy has a ton of unpaid parking tickets, but the address he gave the DMV is an abandoned building."

"Where?"

"South Philly."

"Call Hal and let him know what you found out. I'll swing back by the motel and pick Sophie up so we can pay another visit to Richard Kraft at Walton Creek Middle School. Text me the address of that abandoned building after you talk to Hal. And start running his name through every database you can find."

Liv was getting absolutely nowhere with the receptionist in the school's office and was obviously close to strangling someone. The woman was insisting the vice-principal was in an important budget meeting. Liv tried to threaten her, and Sophie began to re-evaluate her assessment that Liv wasn't bad at dealing with people. She placed a steadying hand on Liv's forearm and squeezed gently.

"This is an emergency," Sophie said calmly, trying to appeal to the woman's sense of duty. "We were here a few days ago, and Mrs. Cunningham told us to get in touch with her if we needed anything else. Will you please let her know Agents Andrews and Kane are here to see her?"

The receptionist glared at Liv as she picked up the phone and punched in three numbers. Sophie let out a breath and pulled Liv away from the desk. Liv relaxed under her touch and seemed to calm a bit.

"Does threatening people usually work for you, Agent Andrews?" she asked quietly.

"Apparently not with civilians." She shrugged. "Thank you for stepping in."

"Thank you for not ripping into me when I interrupted." Sophie pulled her down to sit in a chair just inside the door to the office area. She glanced at the receptionist, who was still on the phone speaking low enough that she couldn't hear what was being said. She returned her attention to Liv and noticed the dark circles under her eyes and her hands shaking slightly. Since their trip back from Philadelphia, Liv had done a good job of keeping the two of them apart, and Sophie hadn't spent more than ten minutes alone in her presence until the day before. "When's the last time you ate?"

"Excuse me?" Liv seemed surprised by the question, but refused to meet her eyes.

"When we're done here, I'm taking you to the diner for some food." She held a hand up and shook her head when Liv opened her mouth to argue. "You need to eat. You've been avoiding me, and you've been neglecting your health. You're eating lunch with me, and I'm not going to fight with you about it."

Liv tensed and no doubt was about to protest, but the receptionist cleared her throat loudly and got their attention.

"Mrs. Cunningham will see you now," she told them, her tone icy. Liv thanked her as they walked by, but the woman glared.

"Let me do the talking, all right?" Sophie asked when they entered the office. Liv nodded, and Sophie turned her attention to the vice-principal.

"I heard someone saw Timmy York yesterday," Mrs. Cunningham said once everyone was seated. "I'm assuming since Richard was here all day yesterday it couldn't have been him. Have you found the man yet?"

"No, we haven't," she said, and glanced over at Liv, who was staring out the window behind the vice-principal, clenching her jaw rapidly. Was it because she was forcing Liv to share a meal with her or was she simply letting everything that had happened the day before get to her? "Mrs. Cunningham, could you tell us what Richard Kraft's middle name is?"

"Oh," she said as she stood and went to a file cabinet. How odd that people still used filing cabinets since most information was kept on computers now. If things weren't so grim, Sophie might have smiled at the nostalgia that washed over her. After a moment, Mrs. Cunningham removed a file and returned to her seat, then pulled a sheet of paper from the file. "Here it is. It appears as though he doesn't have a middle name. There's no initial or anything here."

Liv reached for the paper, and Mrs. Cunningham handed it to her without a word. Sophie sucked in a breath when Liv pointed at the address Kraft had given as his previous place of residence in Philadelphia, which was in the same area as the abandoned building Marcus Kraft was using.

"We need to see Kraft now." Liv's voice was tight, but her tone left no room for argument. The vice-principal picked up her phone and called the receptionist, and Liv and Sophie remained silent while she ordered that Kraft come to her office immediately. Before she even hung up the announcement went out over the public-address system.

"We'll need to speak with him alone, please," Sophie said.

"Of course. I'll just be in the principal's office if you need me." She got up and left the room.

Sophie was glad she hadn't asked what was going on, even though she could see that Mrs. Cunningham wanted desperately to know.

"Mansfield will hang if Kraft is involved in this," Liv said, still staring at the paper.

"Feel free to take over questioning Kraft at any time," Sophie told her. "Threats might actually work with this one."

CHAPTER NINETEEN

Patricia, what's this about? I was in the middle of—" Kraft's mouth shut with a snap as he entered the room and saw them sitting there. Liv stood and faced him as he swallowed loudly. "What's going on here?"

"I was hoping you might be able to tell us," she said. Her calm exterior belied the fury churning in her gut. She sat on the edge of the desk with her arms crossed in front of her. Her eyes never left Kraft's as she spoke. "We're through playing games, Kraft. What do you know about Timmy York's abduction?"

"Nothing." He shut the door behind him before walking farther into the room. "I don't know anything about it, I swear."

"Who's Marcus?" Liv asked. His eyes narrowed slightly, and he glanced at Sophie. His attention returned to Liv as he shoved his hands into his pockets.

"I don't know anyone named Marcus," he said, a touch of defiance in his voice.

"Really? I find that interesting since not only do you share a last name, but the address we have on file for him is in the same neighborhood as the one you gave this school as your place of residence in Philadelphia."

He looked everywhere in the room but at her. When he calmly sat down in the chair she had vacated she wanted to grab him by the shirt front and shake some sense into him, but she somehow managed to stay completely still while he tried to come up with a response. She decided he might need a bit of prodding, so she pushed off the desk and moved to him, leaning over so both hands rested on the arms of his chair. When he finally met her eyes, she saw the fear there. "Are you Marcus Kraft? If you are, I can arrest you now. If you don't want that to happen, then I suggest you start telling us what you know."

"Mark is my cousin," he blurted out suddenly. "Jesus, are you telling me he has something to do with these kids turning up dead?"

Liv studied his face for any telltale signs that he was lying but saw nothing. It appeared as though he really didn't know what was going on, and her anger surged again as she stood up straight. She motioned for Sophie to explain things to him, because she didn't trust the rage steadily growing inside her. Each child that ended up dead seemed like a personal affront to her, and she needed someone to take the anger out on. Richard Kraft could not be that person if he knew anything that might be able to help them rescue Timmy before he met the same fate as Kendra Henderson. She walked to the window while Sophie spoke in her usual calm, soothing manner. Surprisingly some of the tension left her shoulders as she listened to Sophie's rich voice.

"I don't know anything about any of it, I swear," he said when Sophie finished. Liv didn't turn away from the view of the track and field area.

"I don't believe you, Richard," she said, her eyes following a young boy running around the track. "You've already lied to us numerous times, so why should I believe you aren't lying now?"

"What?" he asked, sounding thoroughly confused.

Liv turned and was in front of him so fast he stood and knocked the chair over backward in an attempt to get away from her. He backed up against the wall, and Liv stopped with her nose about an inch from his. His fear let her know that her eyes were conveying the right amount of anger.

"I never lied to you."

"No? The whole Marcus-being-your-cousin thing aside, we find out Timmy York has anger issues, and you show up at work the next day with a bruise under your eye. You tell us you got it when you were hit by a foul ball, but your assistant coach told me you spent the entire practice in your car, on the phone, and never got hit with a ball." Liv was seething, and she didn't notice she was cocking her arm back to hit the man until Sophie was beside her, a hand firmly on the small of her back.

"Let's sit down, shall we?" she asked.

Liv was breathing heavily, and she tore her eyes from Kraft long enough to see the fear in Sophie's eyes. That Sophie might be afraid of her sobered her enough that she backed away from Kraft.

Once calm was restored, Sophie took over the questioning. "Mr. Kraft, if we were to subpoena your phone records, would we find out you were talking to your cousin that afternoon?"

"I want to speak to my lawyer."

Liv met Sophie's eyes and saw her own surprise mirrored there. That was not something she would have expected an innocent man to say.

"You can certainly call your lawyer, but we're just here to talk," Sophie told him.

"She threatened to arrest me," he said, pointing at Liv.

She closed her eyes for a moment to try to calm herself once again.

"We don't have anything to arrest you for, Richard. She was just blowing off steam." Sophie turned the phone on the desk to face him. "We just want to know about Marcus. Have you spoken to him lately?"

"He called me the morning you came here to talk to me." Kraft slumped.

Liv hoped against hope they were finally going to get somewhere with him. She sat in the vice-principal's chair while they waited for him to go on.

He looked back and forth between them nervously. "He told me he'd gotten himself into some kind of trouble, and he didn't know how to get out of it. I met with him yesterday morning at the diner in town, and he was really scared. He wouldn't tell me what was going on, but I'd never seen him like that. I told him if anything illegal was going on, I didn't want any part of it, and I got the hell out of there."

"What time did you meet him at the diner?" Liv asked. Her heart began to race at the prospect of linking Marcus Kraft to Victor's murder.

"About five thirty," he answered.

That would be the right timeframe. She made a note to call Hal for Victor's approximate time of death. She also cursed Mansfield yet again for pulling the tail. A thought occurred to her then—something was very off about Mansfield's explanation of the events. She mentally kicked herself for not catching it earlier.

"What time did you arrive at work yesterday morning?" she asked, her heart beating wildly.

"A little before six thirty. My first class isn't until eight fifteen, but Mark told me he needed to meet with me. When he left, I decided to just come in early and catch up on some stuff."

"Can someone verify that?" Liv asked.

"Mrs. Cunningham was here to oversee morning detention. It starts at seven," he answered with a nod.

She stared at him for a moment before meeting Sophie's eyes and motioning for her to follow her out to the hallway.

"What is it?"

"The night manager at the motel didn't find Vic's body until close to eight in the morning. Mansfield said he was following Kraft to work when the radio call went out." Liv stopped talking when a student walked by. She waited until he was far enough away that he couldn't hear their conversation. "If Kraft was here before six thirty, then Mansfield couldn't have been telling the truth about the sequence of events."

"Maybe he left here when he got the call and backtracked to the motel. Kraft was here for the day, so why stick around?" Sophie was obviously trying to see the situation from both sides, but Liv could tell by the look in her eyes that they were on the same page.

"But why lie about it?" Liv ran a hand through her hair as she tried to quell the rising excitement at possibly getting a break in the case. She pulled her cell phone out and dialed Justin's number. Mansfield might not have gotten that call yet relieving him of his position, but if he had, she hoped to God he hadn't run. If he didn't know they were on to him then maybe—just *maybe*—he'd still be at home. She held Sophie's gaze when Justin answered. "It's Andrews. Is Mansfield still there?"

"No, he left about twenty minutes ago," Justin answered. "He got that phone call you warned him about just after you left."

"Shit." Liv shook her head so Sophie would know he was gone. "Justin, I need someone to hightail it to Mansfield's residence. I want him brought in for questioning. I'll fill you in later. Just make sure he gets back to the station. Hold him in a cell if you have to."

She shoved the phone into her pocket and then held the door open for Sophie to walk back into the office ahead of her. Hopefully Richard could give them a little more information about his cousin Marcus.

"What kind of trouble did he say he was in, Richard?" Sophie asked.

"I told you he wouldn't tell me. He just said it was really bad, and his life was in danger. His mother's life is at stake too."

"Can you tell us where Marcus lives?" Sophie kept encouraging him to talk while Liv pulled a notebook out of her pocket and got ready to write. He gave an address in Philadelphia, informing them that Marcus lived with his mother there. "Is Marcus into drugs, Richard? Anything you can tell us might help us to help him."

"No, as far as I know, he's never done anything more than smoke a joint now and again." Kraft shook his head. "He spent some time in jail for armed robbery a few years ago, and he's been going to the casinos a lot since they started opening up around the state."

Liv knew money lending was a big business for organized crime. Was it possible Marcus Kraft got in over his head a little too far and owed a large amount of money to the wrong people? It certainly wasn't out of the question, but she couldn't figure out where abducting children might factor in with that scenario. Or Robert Mansfield either, for that matter.

"If you hear from him again, we need to know about it immediately, all right?" Sophie handed him a business card, and Liv gave him another of hers as well. He nodded as he looked at the cards. "We want to help him, Richard, but we can't do that if we can't find him."

"I'll call you," he assured her.

"How did you get that bruise under your eye, Richard?" Liv asked.

"One of my students was tossing a book at another kid, and I got in the way." He laughed, but then met Liv's eyes with a serious expression. "I lied because I should have reported the incident, but I didn't see a reason to get the student in trouble."

"Your secret is safe with me as long as you're being honest with us." She motioned to Sophie that they should wrap things up. When Kraft had returned to his classroom, Liv led Sophie out to the parking lot. "Do you believe him?"

"Oddly enough, I do. Are you going to call Hal with this information?"

"I am." Liv pulled out of the parking lot. "Let's track this bastard down."

CHAPTER TWENTY

L unch was forgotten. Liv needed Sophie to man the command center while Justin drove to Philadelphia to check out
Kraft's information. Justin had sent Parsons to pick up Mansfield,
but he wasn't home. His wife was there but said she had no idea
when he'd be back. Liv ordered Parsons to stay there until she could
send someone else out to keep an eye on the house and to get his ass
into the station as soon as he showed his face.

Liv couldn't get the niggling feeling out of her head that
Mansfield was somehow involved in Victor's death, so she went
back to the scene to look around. She'd spent an hour scrutinizing
the area, never able to completely get the image of Victor's lifeless
body out of her mind, when she saw a white button lying on the
ground, mostly covered in blood-stained dirt, and she flashed back
to the day of the murder. *Mansfield's shirt was missing a button.* She
quickly bagged it and took it back to the station, intending to have
someone retrieve the shirt and confirm the button did indeed belong
to Mansfield.

The address Richard Kraft had given them for his cousin panned
out. It belonged to Marcus's mother, but she insisted she hadn't seen
him in more than two months. According to her, he had a job in a
small town in Upper Bucks County, which coincidentally—and Liv
didn't believe in coincidences—was a hell of a lot closer to Walton
Creek than it was to Philadelphia. Justin believed the woman was
telling the truth, but Hal assigned someone to watch her house just

in case she wasn't. She insisted she didn't have a physical address for him though, so they started searching records for him in Upper Bucks County.

Liv held the door to the diner open for Sophie and followed her inside around seven that evening. Liv was surprised to see Peter York in the kitchen, alongside his wife Abby. The hostess came to seat them, but Liv waved her off.

"Do you mind if we just get something to take back to the motel?" she asked Sophie, who simply shook her head. They looked over the menu and placed their orders with the waitress working the counter area. Peter and Abby looked preoccupied, whether with grief or their work, Liv wasn't entirely sure, but she decided not to bother them. She took a seat at the counter and asked for a cup of coffee.

"I feel like we should say something to them." Sophie took the stool to Liv's right and nodded at the waitress when she held the coffee pot up in a silent question.

"That's probably not a good idea." Liv took a sip of her coffee, welcoming the burn down her throat that reminded her she was alive. She'd been having a tough time getting the images of Kendra Henderson out of her mind. She hoped that wasn't a harbinger of what would happen to Timmy if they didn't find him soon.

"Agent Andrews."

Liv turned her head to meet Peter's steady gaze. He looked at Sophie and nodded. "Your meals are on the house. For as long as you're in town."

"That really isn't necessary," Liv said. The rest of her protest died on her lips at the intense grief that clouded his eyes for no more than a second. So much emotion welled in her chest she had to look away from him.

"Please," he said, his voice choked. "I wasn't the easiest person to deal with when you came to speak with us the night Timmy was abducted. I know you were only doing what was necessary to find our son, and I truly appreciate everything you've done for us, especially yesterday in the search for his body. I don't need to tell you how happy I am he wasn't there. Please let me do this for you. To show my appreciation for all that you people in law enforcement do."

Liv didn't know how to react. The tears that threatened to fall were so not like her. Not trusting her voice at that moment, she nodded her agreement.

"We will find your son," she said, hoping it wasn't a lie.

He grasped her arm briefly before walking back into the kitchen. She took a deep breath and stared into her coffee cup, feeling Sophie's eyes on her, but she refused to look at her. She wouldn't cry in front of anyone, especially the one person who seemed to be able to look past her rough façade and see her for the woman she wanted to be.

❖

Mark's heart was beating fast and he was unusually hot. He'd put the window down but that didn't seem to be helping. A glance at his watch told him the van would be pulling up any minute. The phone call that morning had gone better than he'd expected. He was being given one last opportunity to prove himself. If he handed off the girl the next afternoon, all would be forgiven. He had no idea why, but he knew enough not to question his seeming good fortune.

In fact, the conversation went *too* well. It was *too* easy. That probably was the calm before the storm, as his mother always said, and he was desperate for this one to go according to plan so he could have some bargaining power.

He'd gotten Timmy established back in the basement of the house, and now Mark sat in his truck outside Walmart waiting. He might not have been the smartest man ever born, but it would be a bad idea to take one abducted child with him to grab another.

He'd been coming here every night for the past two weeks, watching the same scene play out. She'd drive up, run inside to let her husband know she was there to pick him up when his shift ended, and be back out in less than two minutes. Even though the store was open twenty-four hours, there was never much traffic at night. He'd have to be quick to be able to get the girl out of the van and back to his truck before the mother emerged from the store.

He got out and opened the tailgate to make it look like he was putting purchases away when the minivan pulled up outside the front entrance. The woman jumped out and dashed inside. He made his move before anyone else could pull into the parking lot and see him.

The side door was unlocked and he said a silent thank you. The girl was asleep so he quickly released the seat belt and removed the entire car seat. He noticed a tattered teddy bear on the backseat so he grabbed it. He didn't bother to shut the door, but instead ran back to his truck and set the seat on the floor in front of the passenger seat. He was pulling out of the lot when he looked in his rearview mirror and saw the mother come out of the store.

He smiled at his luck. He was getting good at this. The thought sobered him, and he tried to push it out of his head before it could scare the hell out of him.

Sophie dropped her foam take-out container in the trash and sat back in her chair. She watched Liv as she finished her food. They hadn't talked as they ate, and Sophie was getting tired of trying to deny her attraction to Liv. She wanted to know more about her. Hell, she wanted to know *everything* about her. She was drawn to Liv, and she didn't want to fight her feelings. She respected Liv's stance on not getting involved, but that didn't mean the sound of her voice would stop sending a thrill down Sophie's spine. And it wouldn't stop the jolt of electricity when Liv touched her—inadvertent or not.

"Tell me about your parents." Liv stiffened and said nothing at first when she tossed her container into the trash can. Sophie was about to apologize for being nosy when Liv finally began to talk.

"I told you about them last night," she said.

"Not them. The Andrewses. The people who adopted you."

"They live in Chicago, which is where I grew up. Kyle is a doctor, and Janet is a high-school teacher." Liv was looking down at her hands, and Sophie knew she wouldn't continue without prodding. It was almost as though she wanted to make sure Sophie really wanted to hear what she had to say.

"They changed your life." Sophie purposely phrased the words as a statement rather than a question. She didn't look away when Liv raised her eyes to hers.

"They made me realize I was actually worth something. That the crap I'd dealt with growing up in the foster system wasn't normal. I truly felt loved for the first time in my life." Liv focused on some point on the wall behind Sophie's head. "I sure as hell didn't make things easy on them for the first few weeks. I fought their affection for me tooth and nail. I was afraid that if I let myself care about them, they'd abandon me like everyone else had."

Sophie wanted to tell her she didn't need to be alone, that she *was* worth something. But this wasn't the time or place. She was hopelessly attracted to Liv and guessed Liv was seriously drawn to her as well. The problem was Liv's strict rule of not getting involved with someone she worked with. As long as they were on the case together, Sophie had to bite her tongue.

"I've always kept people—especially women—from getting to know me very well because of that fear," Liv said. "If I'm the one to leave first, then I can't be hurt."

"That seems like a fatalistic attitude," Sophie said quietly. Her heart ached for everything Liv had endured while she was growing up. "I believe there's someone out there for everyone. You just need to be open to the possibilities."

"Jesus, Hal's saddled me with a romantic." Liv's smile looked pained. "I used to believe I would find someone who could be everything to me. Someone who would be more important to me than the job. I've pretty much given up on that fantasy though."

"I've had the same issues, but I can't give up. I know someone out there can understand what I do and not hold it against me when the job takes precedence over everything else." Someone like you, she wanted to say. It was getting increasingly difficult as they spent time together to not touch Liv. The way her green eyes danced when she was teasing, and the way the corner of her mouth would twitch when she looked at her. All of those things were conspiring to wear down Sophie's resolve.

"You need to talk to Parsons and let her know you aren't interested."

Sophie stared at her for a moment, wondering where the change in conversation came from.

"Excuse me?"

"I've seen the way she follows you around like a lost puppy," Liv said. "You need to nip it in the bud before she starts to think she has a chance with you."

"What makes you think I'm not interested?" Sophie was angry and didn't really understand why. Liv was right, but what business was it of hers? Liv had made it perfectly clear there would never be more than friendship between them, so why was she trying to dictate who she got involved with?

"Are you?"

"No," Sophie said before she could stop the word from leaving her mouth. Damn it, it would have been nice to see where the jealousy bit might have gone.

"Then why are we arguing about it?"

She shook her head and began to make her way across the room to the bathroom. Distance from Liv was what she needed right now. She was almost there when Liv gripped her forearm and she turned to face her.

Liv's pupils dilated when their eyes met, and Sophie bit back a moan when she saw Liv's lips part and her tongue dart out to moisten her lips. Liv was going to kiss her, and she wanted her to. She would die if Liv *didn't* kiss her.

"We can't do this, Liv," she whispered, but her words lacked conviction. She didn't protest when Liv's hand slid up her arm to her neck. "I won't be able to stop at a kiss."

"That's good, because I don't want you to."

"What do you want from me?" Sophie regretted the question as soon as the words were out of her mouth.

Liv pulled back, breaking their connection. "Has anyone ever told you that you talk too much?"

"I get that occasionally." She took a step toward Liv and put a hand to her cheek when she didn't back away. "It doesn't matter if all you can offer is tonight, Liv, but I need you to kiss me before I combust."

"We can't have that, can we?" Liv lowered her head to kiss her, but stopped less than an inch from her lips. She stared into Sophie's eyes, and Sophie almost whimpered at the anticipation building inside her. "Are you sure?"

Sophie didn't answer with words, but moved her hand to the back of Liv's neck and pulled her closer, eliminating the distance between them. Her eyes fluttered closed at the first touch of Liv's incredibly soft lips. She couldn't stop the moan of pleasure when Liv's tongue ran across her lips, demanding entrance. Liv's hands were on her hips, pulling her body tight against hers, and Sophie gave in to the demands, relishing the rush of liquid fire between her legs when Liv's tongue found hers. She fisted her hand in Liv's hair, holding her close as the kiss deepened. Liv's hips had begun to grind against her when Sophie had to break the kiss. Not because she wanted to, but because she needed to breathe. She rested her forehead against Liv's shoulder and gasped.

"Damn, I should have known someone as intense as you would be a fantastic kisser." Sophie was happy to hear Liv's ragged breaths too. "That was even better than the last time."

"Take your clothes off," Liv said, her mouth hot against Sophie's ear.

Sophie held tighter to her when Liv sucked her earlobe gently. She moved her hands to the hem of Liv's shirt, but instead of lifting it up and over her head, she ran her hands up Liv's sides, causing a delicious tremble to course through Liv's body.

"Please. I need you naked. Now." Liv tugged insistently at Sophie's shirt.

Sophie stepped back but faltered at the pure desire in Liv's eyes. No one had ever looked at her like that—like she was the only woman in the world. Her breath caught in her throat and she was about to remove her shirt when Liv's cell phone rang.

CHAPTER TWENTY-ONE

This better be important, Justin," Liv said, raking a hand through her hair with thinly veiled impatience.

"Where the hell are you and Kane?" Hal Davidson asked. Liv pulled the phone away from her ear and checked the number again. It was definitely Justin's.

"Why are you calling from his number? And why are you in Walton Creek?" Liv asked. She shook her head at Sophie, who was looking at her worriedly.

"I came to try and figure out what happened to my agent, Andrews." He sighed, and Liv heard in his tone how distressed he was. "And a four-year-old girl was abducted from a parking lot in Upper Bucks County about thirty minutes ago. Is that important enough for you?"

"Fuck." Liv sat down on her bed and searched the bedside table for a pen and paper. "Give me everything we know."

When she hung up with him, she looked at Sophie, who was sitting on her own bed facing her. This was not how she wanted the night to end. While they were eating dinner, all she could think about was getting into bed with Sophie and waking up in her arms after a night of what she was sure would be incredibly satisfying sex. She reached across the space between the two beds and gently rubbed her palm along Sophie's thigh. Sophie could obviously read the disappointment in her eyes, because she took Liv's hand and gave her a devious grin.

"A rain check, yes?" Sophie asked. "I'm assuming we have another abduction."

Liv felt something inside her click into place. She'd never been with anyone who was okay with sex being interrupted by a phone call about work. She smiled and bent over when she stood, planting a kiss on Sophie's lips.

"Just don't think you've dodged a bullet, Agent Andrews. I fully intend to finish what was started here, just as soon as possible."

"I wouldn't expect anything less, Agent Kane." She threw Sophie her FBI windbreaker before grabbing her own. "And my boss is here now. So be on your best behavior, all right? And this never happened as far as anyone else is concerned. Especially Hal."

"Understood."

Hal, Gabe, and Justin had gotten a bit of a head start on them, so they were already working the scene when Liv pulled up behind a cruiser. The parking-lot lights did little to illuminate the vast majority of the area, and the flashing lights from the surrounding cruisers cast an eerie glow. Liv shoved through the crowd of onlookers, badge in hand, to where Justin stood with a uniformed officer.

"What do we know?" she asked, clapping a hand on his shoulder.

"The mother is over there." He pointed toward the store's entrance, where Liv saw a woman seated on the ground, her face wet with tears and looking like she was in shock. She was surrounded by people, at least two of them uniforms. "Four-year-old girl named Katie McCoy. The kid was sleeping in the backseat, and the mother ran in to let her husband know she was here to pick him up from work. She says she was only inside for a couple of minutes, but the girl was gone when she came back out."

"Did anybody see anything?" Liv knew the question was pointless. There were never any witnesses. People either didn't want to get involved or walked around so blinkered they never saw what was going on in front of them.

"Nothing," Justin said.

"Why does that not surprise me?" She glanced at the mother again and was glad to see Sophie making her way over to get her official statement. Liv turned her attention to the building's exterior walls and the fixtures illuminating the parking lot. "Cameras?"

"Only two, and one is trained solely on the entrance. Hal and Frank are upstairs with security now taking a quick look at what they have."

She stepped away from Justin when her phone rang. It was Frank, calling from the security office. They'd seen someone suspicious on the surveillance video Hal wanted her to look at. Before hurrying inside, she gave Justin instructions to send Sophie up there as soon as she finished speaking with the child's mother.

❖

"Please, you need to find my little girl," Susannah McCoy said to Sophie. She was clutching her husband Ryan's arm and they both seemed in shock. The mother was crying and the father kept wiping away tears from his own cheeks.

"That's our goal," Sophie said in her most reassuring tone. "Are you sure you didn't see anyone out here? Either when you got out of the car or when you came back?"

"No one," she said again, shaking her head as she spoke. "God, I just run inside so he knows I'm here to pick him up and come right back out. I've been doing it for months."

Sophie wrote everything down and looked into Susannah's eyes. This woman was truly heartbroken. No one could fake that. She put her notebook away and took the other woman's hands.

"Can you recall anything to help us find this guy? Even if you don't think it's important. Maybe you saw someone suspicious in recent days? Please think."

She shook her head, but then something seemed to dawn on her. She tugged on her husband's arm and looked at him. "Remember the other night I told you about the man who was out here when I came back to the car?" she asked.

"Yes. You said he was looking in the car and talked to you about Katie."

"What about her?" Sophie asked. She pulled out her notebook again and got ready to write more.

"He said how sweet she looked sleeping in the backseat. I didn't think anything of it at the time. He seemed nice enough, and I didn't get the sense he was up to something, but maybe he was," Susannah said.

"Can you recall what he looked like?" Sophie asked. Susannah closed her eyes but shook her head after a moment.

"He was so ordinary. Nothing stood out about him," she said, looking like she would start crying again. "Wait, yes, there was something. He had a tattoo. I couldn't see it very well because he had his shirt sleeves down, but it was on his right forearm."

"That's good," Sophie said with a nod. "Anything else? Hair color, height—anything you can remember would be helpful."

"He was about Ryan's size," she said, looking at her husband. She appeared apologetic when she turned back to Sophie. "I really can't recall much. Oh, God, my baby." She started sobbing again and buried her face in her husband's shoulder.

"That's okay, you did great, Susannah. One more thing. Did you notice what kind of car he was driving? Or if there were any cars in the parking lot tonight when you got here?

She closed her eyes for a moment. "A truck. I'm sorry, I didn't even look at it, really. But I saw a truck here both times."

As Sophie wrote, her adrenaline surged. "That's great, thank you. If you remember anything else that might help us, please don't hesitate to call. We're going to do everything in our power to bring your little girl back home."

Sophie turned and motioned for Justin to join them. They walked a few feet away from the McCoys and Sophie relayed everything she'd found out from them.

"That's not really much to go on," he said, his doubt evident in his tone. "I'll make sure they get out of here all right. Liv wants you to join her upstairs in the security office. She, Hal, and Frank are up there looking at surveillance tapes."

"Thanks," Sophie said before she rejoined the McCoys to give them a few more words of encouragement. When Justin ushered them away from the chaos of police cruisers, Sophie headed inside the store.

❖

It was a little after midnight when the store manager led her into the security office. Liv was hunkered down in front of a monitor with Frank sitting right next to her.

"What do we have?" she asked. Frank stood and offered her his seat, which she gladly took. Liv never looked away from the screen, but pointed at a man who was just approaching the entrance to the store. Sophie watched as he glanced up at the camera, then hurriedly looked away again. "Oh, my God. Richard Kraft."

"That's what I thought at first too, but look," Liv said. After pausing the video she pointed at the man's forearm. Sophie moved closer and saw an elaborate tattoo of a dragon encircling his forearm. Kraft had been wearing a short-sleeved shirt on both occasions they'd met with him, and he had no such tattoo.

"His cousin Marcus?" Sophie asked.

"It has to be." Liv jumped up and began to pace. "No wonder Patricia Cunningham thought she was looking at Richard when she saw the convenience-store tape on television. They could almost be twins."

"The mother, Susannah McCoy, said she spoke with a man a few nights ago who had a tattoo on his right forearm," Sophie said, unable to take her eyes away from the monitor. "This has to be him. He actually made contact with her beforehand."

"Excuse me, ma'am. I was told you had a question for me?" the store manager said. He was a rather nerdy-looking young man, probably in his mid-twenties, with thick glasses and a pocket protector filled with an array of pens.

"Do you know this man?" Liv asked, indicating the still-paused video.

He looked so flustered Sophie almost felt sorry for him. She glanced at Hal and was surprised that he was just sitting back, almost like he was observing. Sophie thought he would've taken over the investigation.

"No," he said, but then squinted at the screen. "Wait a minute. I've seen that tat before."

"But you don't know who he is?" Sophie asked. She glanced at his name tag briefly. "Kurt, are you sure you don't know him?"

He was obviously deep in thought as he stared at the image and used a finger to push his glasses up his nose. Sophie wanted to shake him to make him respond. After a moment he snapped his fingers and turned to the store's head of security.

"You remember about a week ago when that old lady came in complaining about some weird guy hanging around the entrance?" he asked.

"I was on vacation a week ago," the guy answered.

"Oh, yeah," Kurt mumbled as he scratched the back of his neck. He turned to look at Sophie. "I had to go out and ask him to get lost because he was making my customers nervous."

"And you're sure it was this guy?" she asked.

"I can't really say I remember his face, but I definitely remember his ink," he said with a nod. "It was wicked cool. I asked him where he got it done."

"Where?" Liv asked, obviously losing her patience with Kurt. He looked at her like he didn't know what she was asking. Liv looked at Sophie for help.

"Where did he say he got it done?" she asked calmly. If they could find out where, they might be able to get a current address.

"Some place in Philly, but I don't remember the name. Sorry," he said with a shrug.

"You didn't happen to get his name, did you?" Liv asked.

Liv stopped pacing and gripped the back of a chair like she was holding on for dear life. Was she imagining the chair was Kurt's neck?

"I asked him to leave, and I assume he did. I didn't have a conversation with him."

"You never went back out to check?" Sophie asked. Kurt shook his head and looked apologetic. "Don't you have paperwork you have to fill out when there's a complaint?"

"Yeah, but he said he was gonna leave. No harm, no foul, right?"

"In basketball, yes, in life, no," Hal muttered from his spot in the back of the room.

"What time of day was this?" Liv asked through clenched teeth.

"I work three to midnight, and I think it was right after I got back from my dinner break," he said, looking up at the ceiling and apparently trying to capture memories of the night in question. "It had to have been between eight thirty and nine."

Liv whipped her head around to meet Sophie's gaze.

"Pretty much the same time as the abduction," Liv said quietly. He'd obviously been coming to this store waiting for some unsuspecting mother to leave her child in the car while she went inside for something.

"Fuck, Liv," Sophie muttered. "The mother says she's been coming here to pick her husband up every night he's worked for the past couple of months. She insists she didn't do anything differently tonight than she did before."

"He was targeting her then," Liv said. She wanted more than anything to catch Marcus Kraft and make him pay for the hell he'd caused so many families. "He knew exactly how long she'd be in the store, and how much time he had to grab the kid before someone would spot him." She looked back at the monitor, which was paused to show his face looking directly into the camera. "He even knew where the cameras were and was well aware they wouldn't pick him up while he was actually committing the crime."

"What now?" Frank asked from the office doorway.

"I want this bastard's name and face in every newspaper and on every television station in a hundred-and-fifty-mile radius by morning," Liv said.

Frank nodded and ran out of the office. Hal left the office too, and Liv turned to Sophie, a twinge of regret in her gut that they wouldn't be finishing what they'd started earlier anytime soon. "We're going to wake up Richard Kraft and find out what the hell is going on."

CHAPTER TWENTY-TWO

I swear I don't know," Kraft told them for the hundredth time since their arrival at almost two in the morning. "I haven't heard from him since yesterday morning. He didn't tell me where he was living. He said it was too dangerous for me to know."

"His mother says she doesn't have his address either," Liv told him, failing to keep her aggravation at bay. They were so close to catching him, but he was somehow managing to stay just off their radar. "I'm having a hard time believing neither of you knows where he is, Richard. Somebody needs to start telling us the truth before one of these kids turns up dead."

"I swear," he said again, looking like he was about to cry. "And my aunt wouldn't lie to you about Mark. I think she's afraid of him. If she knew where he was, she'd tell you."

Liv closed her eyes and took a deep breath. Her gut told her he was being honest. Sophie's hand closed around her wrist, and utter calm came over her. She opened her eyes but refused to look at Sophie. If she did, her need would be obvious to everyone in the room.

"If I find out you've lied to us—again—you'll be going to jail for obstruction of justice. You know that, right?" Liv was amazed that she was able to keep her voice even. Kraft nodded and glanced at his wife, who was sitting silently by his side.

Liv didn't know what to do. She couldn't arrest him, because as far as she could tell, he'd done nothing wrong. They'd even agreed to let her put surveillance equipment on their home phone. They were cooperating fully, and Liv's need to catch Marcus was growing stronger with each second. She was sure he'd try to get in touch with Richard again, because it sounded to her like everything was falling apart for him. He was clearly scared and looking for a way out. Richard was the lifeline he would reach for.

They waited until a uniformed officer arrived on the doorstep before leaving the Krafts' home. Richard didn't believe his cousin posed a threat to him and his wife, but Liv wasn't so sure. Come morning, his name and face would be plastered everywhere, and there was no telling what he would do when he felt cornered.

❖

"Listen up," Liv said when she walked into the station after leaving Richard Kraft's home. The entire team was there now, plus Hal, and minus Victor. She took a deep breath and forced herself not to think about him. "I need to bounce some ideas off you guys. I think I know what happened to Victor."

"What?" Frank asked as everyone paid attention.

"Wrong place, wrong time," Liv said with a shake of her head. "Richard Kraft says he met with his cousin Marcus around five thirty in the morning. Justin, you said Vic left around five. Could it have been closer to five thirty?"

"Yeah, it could have."

"Okay, stay with me, guys," Liv moved to the dry-erase board at the front of the room and picked up the marker. "Hal, I'm assuming you have autopsy results? What was the time of death for Victor?"

"Between four thirty and six thirty a.m.," Hal answered, after looking at his notes. Liv wrote the time down on the board and turned back to him.

"All right, I'm going to assume Marcus took Timmy with him to meet Richard at the diner. I think Victor saw the kid in the car and realized he'd found the kidnapper."

"Holy shit. So he took Victor and killed him so he couldn't ID him." Justin looked pale and tired, and Liv knew she needed to get him to see a shrink when they got back so he didn't carry Victor's death on his shoulders for the rest of his life.

"There's a couple of things wrong with your theory, Liv," Sophie said. All eyes turned to her, and Liv silently thanked her for speaking up. She didn't want to be the one to accuse another cop—at least not on her own. "Mansfield said he was tailing Richard and pulled off when he heard the call about a body being found. If that was true, wouldn't he have seen whatever happened to Victor? Assuming, of course, he was there while Richard met with Marcus."

"Good point." Liv nodded and smiled as she opened the door to the squad room. "Winters, get in here please."

A young male officer followed her into the conference room looking terrified. He glanced at all the FBI agents sitting around the table and paled.

"Yes, ma'am?"

"You were assigned to tail Richard Kraft on the overnight shifts, correct?" Liv asked. Winters nodded and shifted his weight from one foot to the other. "Were you doing that yesterday morning?"

"Until about four thirty," he answered. "Sergeant Mansfield relieved me then and told me to go home to get some rest."

"Was that his usual routine? To relieve you that early in the morning?" Liv had already spoken to Winters about it all when he'd reported to work that afternoon. She was only asking now so the rest of the team could hear it from his own mouth, not just from her.

"No, ma'am. He normally wouldn't do that until seven, at least. It was always after Kraft had arrived at work for the day." He cleared his throat when Liv turned back to her team. "Excuse me, ma'am?"

"Stop calling me that, Winters," she said. "What is it?"

"We still haven't been able to find him. He hasn't returned home."

"Andrews, what the hell's going on?" Hal asked.

"I told you to stay with me." She grinned as a rush of adrenaline coursed through her. "When I was with Mansfield yesterday morning, I noticed he was missing a button from his shirt. I didn't really think anything of it at the time, but I went back there this morning and found it. Right underneath where Victor's head had been. If anyone has an explanation as to how that could have happened without Mansfield being there *before* Vic was shot, I'm all ears."

"It was Mansfield?" Frank asked, a dazed look in his eyes. A cop never wanted to believe another cop was capable of committing murder.

"But how?" Gabe asked, sounding every bit as stunned as Frank.

"All right, here's my theory," she said before dismissing Winters and taking a seat at the table. "Mansfield was at the diner because he was tailing Richard. Richard was meeting with his cousin Marcus, and I'm assuming the kid was in Marcus's car since Timmy was seen not long after that in Forks Township. Victor pulls into the lot and goes inside to get some food. Now, because my theory hinges on the belief that Mansfield is somehow involved in the kidnappings, he worries that Victor might see the kid. While Victor's inside the diner, he sabotages Justin's car so it won't start and figures if Vic doesn't see Timmy, he can simply offer him a ride back to the station. But if Vic does notice the kid, then the ride back is really a ride to the motel, where Mansfield takes him behind the building and kills him. Victor wouldn't have thought twice about getting a ride with Mansfield. None of us would have, had we been in the same position."

"But if he did see the kid, then why wouldn't he have just called, Liv?" Hal asked. "I have to believe he would have done that above anything else, even getting into the car and heading back here. He wouldn't have left the kid there."

"You're right. He wouldn't," Liv said. That was the point in her theory that bothered her the most. She could only think of one reason why he wouldn't have called her or Justin, and it made her stomach churn. "Not unless Mansfield was there with a gun on him. That would mean he intended from the moment he saw him to kill Victor. He wanted a diversion so Kraft could dump Timmy's body, and he got one. Hence the anonymous phone call to the Yorks about their son being found."

"You think Mansfield made that call?" Hal asked.

"If Kraft was supposed to kill Timmy and dump his body at the airport, obviously something changed his mind, and he didn't go through with it. Maybe he got spooked or someone was around." Liv knew she was grasping at straws, but she was following a gut feeling. And her gut very rarely let her down.

"Why the hell isn't he here then?" Hal asked as he stood. "And what does he have to do with the abductions?"

"This entire department is working on that as we speak. I have a unit outside his house waiting for him to show up," Liv said. "We haven't been able to locate him."

"If Mansfield is involved with all of this, how can you be certain his entire department isn't compromised?" Hal paced as he ran a hand through his hair.

"Funny thing about that, Hal," Liv said as she put the marker down. "I've found out no one in this department likes the man. I think he was acting entirely on his own."

"If you're right about this, I'll kill the bastard myself," Frank said as he stood and grabbed his jacket. "I'm going to find him and haul his ass in for an interrogation."

"No, Frank. You're staying here to man the phones," Hal said. Liv silently thanked him, because she'd hate to think what might happen if Frank went after Mansfield alone. "Andrews and Lloyd, you two go. Kane, I want you to finish your report from your interview with the mother from tonight's abduction, then go back to the motel for a couple hours of sleep."

"What about me?" Justin asked, looking from Liv to Hal uncertainly.

"You grab a couple hours now, because I have a feeling none of us is going to get much sleep until Marcus Kraft is in custody," Liv said.

❖

"Damn it!" Liv yelled when they'd gotten back in the car after discovering Mansfield had made a hasty move since she'd had him suspended the day before. They had enough evidence to get a warrant, but when they'd busted into his house, it was empty. They found furniture, but no computers, and the closets were mostly cleared out, which told Liv that Mansfield and his wife had left in a hurry. He must have known it would only be a matter of time before they put two and two together. Infuriatingly, he was probably really there when Parsons had gone to his house. He and the wife must have gone out the back door before they'd had a chance to get a second unit out there. She glanced at her watch and grimaced. It was almost daylight. When was the last time she'd slept?

"We'll find him, Boss," Gabe said with more conviction than Liv was feeling. "He doesn't strike me as being too smart. He'll have left a trail somewhere."

"I hope you're right, Gabe," Liv said, "because this asshole is seriously beginning to piss me off. And I'm tempted to let Frank loose to find him."

Gabe had to know she was just venting, and she wouldn't actually do that, but damn, the visual was appealing.

CHAPTER TWENTY-THREE

Sophie had just gotten into the car to head back to the station after sleeping for about an hour when her cell vibrated on her hip. She didn't recognize the number but answered anyway, since she'd given her number to so many people in the past few days. She said a silent prayer that this call would lead them to their suspect.

"Agent Kane," she said, with only a cursory attempt to hide her exhaustion. It was almost six in the morning, and she couldn't remember the last time she'd gotten more than a few hours of sleep.

"This is Richard Kraft. I just hung up with Mark. He wants me to meet him at a diner in Easton."

"Where?" Sophie's heart sped up and she suddenly felt wide-awake again. She grabbed a piece of paper and a pen from the glove box and wrote down the Tic-Toc Diner on Northampton and Twenty-Fifth Street. When she was done writing she pulled out of the parking lot and sped down the road headed toward Easton. "When?"

"As soon as I can get there," he answered. "I can't have this cop follow me there though. Mark knows you guys are looking for him, and he'll freak out if I show up with a tail."

"I'll be there as soon as I can, Richard. Keep him there until you see me. I'll follow him when the two of you are through talking, because we need to find out where he's living. Let me talk to the officer who's there with you now."

Sophie disconnected after talking to the uniformed cop and telling him to stay well behind Richard, not allowing himself to be seen. She immediately dialed Liv's cell and grew impatient when it rang for the fourth time. She ended the call without waiting for her voice mail to come on and cursed under her breath as she tossed the phone onto the passenger side. It bounced off the seat and landed on the floor. She'd have time to get in touch with Liv once she found the diner.

❖

Liv checked her phone when she was done in the shower and saw she'd missed a call from Sophie. It was almost six thirty, and she had been worried when she'd arrived to an empty motel room but assumed Sophie couldn't sleep and headed back to work. She hit the button to phone her back but it went directly to voice mail. She hung up and pushed the speed-dial for Frank instead, who was still working at the station.

"Hey, Boss," he said.

"Let me talk to Sophie."

"She's not here. Hal sent her to the motel to grab some sleep, remember?"

"I'm at the motel, and she isn't. She tried to call me twenty minutes ago, but I was in the shower." Liv tucked the phone between her shoulder and her ear as she hurried to get dressed. "You're sure she hasn't been there?"

"I'm positive. I've been right here since you and Gabe left to get Mansfield."

"I'll be there in five minutes. Do me a favor and keep trying her cell."

"You got it, Boss."

Liv raked a hand through her hair before sitting down to tie her shoes. Dread settled in the pit of her stomach, and no matter how convincing the voice in her head was when it told her Sophie was fine, she couldn't shake it.

❖

Sophie remained in her vehicle in the diner's parking lot, her eyes trained on the table next to the window where she could see Richard talking to a man she assumed was his cousin Marcus. She reached down quickly to grab her phone, but realized the back had come off when it hit the floor and the battery was gone. The cop she'd told to shadow Richard wasn't visible, just as she'd instructed him.

"Fuck," she muttered. She looked back at the building and panicked when the table was empty. Scanning the perimeter she sighed in relief when she saw the two men walking out the front door. Marcus was looking around like he was expecting a SWAT team to descend on the parking lot. Richard glanced her way and she silently pleaded with him to not give her away. She needed to call Liv, but she couldn't take time to find the battery. Marcus was obviously too nervous to hang around in one spot for very long.

After he climbed into his green pickup truck, she started her engine when he was waiting to move out into traffic. She took a moment to acknowledge she was making a rookie mistake by following him with no backup—especially after what had happened to Victor—but what choice did she have? She tried not to think about how many things could go wrong and pulled out to follow him.

Twenty minutes later he finally turned into a driveway so obscured by plants just beginning to bloom she would never have found it if she'd been looking for it on her own. She drove a few hundred feet farther, pulled off the road, cut the engine immediately, and checked the mirrors to make sure he wasn't coming before she took a moment to search under the seat for her cell-phone battery.

Liv sounded frantic when she answered. "Jesus, Kane, where the hell are you?"

"Kraft called me earlier. I just followed Marcus to his house." Sophie wanted to be happy with the knowledge Liv was worried about her, but she managed to push that thought to the back of her mind. She needed to stay sharp now. She looked at the GPS and was able to give Liv the road she was on, but not the street number. "We were on this road for about ten miles, and I never saw any houses. He lives out in the middle of nowhere."

"You stay where you are, Kane, do you understand me? You are *not* to play the hero and go in looking for those kids. Justin and I are on our way, and we can formulate a plan when we get there. I will not lose another agent on my watch, understood?"

"Understood." She turned in her seat and looked back toward the driveway he had turned into. They hung up with that agreement, but as soon as Sophie shut her phone off and put it in her pocket she got out of the car and made her way back to the house. She crouched at the end of the driveway, knowing she wasn't visible from the house because of the trees and shrubbery along the roadway. She fully intended to stay there and wait for Liv but flinched when she heard a loud crash from the direction of the house. She had to believe Katie and Timmy were in immediate danger. Things were escalating. An agent was dead and another child had been abducted in the span of a couple of days. She couldn't sit there and just wait—she'd go crazy wondering what was happening. She hoped Liv would understand why she'd disobeyed a direct order.

She had plenty of cover to conceal her from any windows in the house so she easily approached without being seen. Her back was against the house, and she had her gun in her hand as she crept toward the back door. She was almost there when she heard the dogs barking from the garage. They sounded small—puppies maybe. She recalled witness information about Timmy being seen with a man and a puppy. She held her breath and waited for him to come out of the house to see what the commotion was about, but after a minute or two she realized he wasn't going to. She let out a sigh of relief before she moved on.

She was moving past the door in a crouch when she saw a window low on the house—obviously a basement. She tried to look through it but it was covered in black paint. She was about to stand again when she heard a noise behind her. A footstep. Before she could spin around to protect herself, white-hot pain flashed through her head and the world disappeared.

❖

"Fuck," Liv said under her breath when she didn't see anyone in her SUV, which Sophie had driven to follow Kraft. Sophie had done a good job of describing where the driveway was, so she and Justin doubled back, guns drawn. She motioned for him to stop as she pulled out her cell phone. She was hoping Sophie had called and she'd somehow missed it, but there was nothing. She couldn't get in touch with her now without possibly giving away Sophie's location. She shoved the phone into her pocket and pointed back toward Justin's car. Liv might have been reckless, but she sure as hell didn't have a death wish. They ran back and retrieved their Kevlar vests.

"Backup's almost here," Justin said, his voice low. "Where do you think she is?"

"Hopefully just out checking the perimeter." Liv couldn't allow herself to believe anything else. She didn't want to lose *another* team member—especially one she was developing serious feelings for. She shook her head to dispel those thoughts, needing her mind clear and sharp. Sophie was missing in action, at least for the moment, and the bastard had those two kids somewhere in the house. Her phone vibrated in her pocket and she quickly pulled it out, her pulse slowing slightly when she saw Sophie's number displayed. "Thank God you're all right. Where are you?"

There was silence from the other end, and Liv's heart dropped when she heard someone breathing. Definitely a man.

"Who is this?" Liv asked. Justin's head whipped around at her words, and he flipped his gun's safety off.

"I think you already know my name, so why don't you tell me yours?"

"Olivia Andrews, FBI. Marcus, where is Agent Kane?"

"She's sleeping right now. She's alive, so don't get any bright ideas about busting in here. I can change her condition before you make it through the front door."

"What about Timmy and Katie?" Liv glanced toward the house, hoping to see him peeking out a window. She also hoped referring to them by name might remind him those kids were real people with families frantic to find them.

"They're here too. The girl was supposed to be picked up this afternoon, but you idiots have ruined everything. Why couldn't you just have stayed away for a few more hours?"

"Marcus, listen to me. We want to help you. Your cousin told us you're in some kind of trouble. What kind of trouble are you in?"

Liv flinched at the sudden dial tone.

"Fuck!"

"Liv, what's going on?"

"The bastard has her. He says she's *sleeping.* If anything happens to her—"

"Nothing will, Boss." Justin's jaw clenched and he shook his head. "We'll get him before he even knows what's happening."

"How long until backup arrives?"

"They were about fifteen minutes behind us. I'd expect this place will be crawling with cops in another five minutes or so."

Liv sat back on her haunches and took a deep breath. It took every ounce of willpower she could muster to not storm the house on her own.

Chapter Twenty-four

L ady," a child's voice was saying from somewhere in the distance. Sophie was vaguely aware of a hand gripping her shoulder and shaking her gently. "Lady, wake up."

Sophie opened her eyes and immediately closed them again. Her head was pounding. It actually felt like it might explode. She had no idea where she was, but it was damp. She held her breath when she heard a rustling noise to her right. Was he back? She'd never been much for religion, but she found herself praying that Liv was out there somewhere. Coming to her rescue. How stupid she'd been to not listen when Liv told her to stay in the car. She promised whatever powers may be that she would always follow orders, if only she got out of this alive.

"Hello?" a meek little voice asked. Sophie's eyes flew open and she willed herself to keep them open as dizziness threatened to make her vomit. She turned her head slowly in the direction of the voice and squinted. It was too dark to make out anything other than shapes in the shadows. The hand was still on her shoulder on her other side.

"Lady, you're awake." The voice sounded relieved. The hand moved away from her and she heard a child begin to cry.

"Hello." She slowly got her bearings. "Are you Timmy and Katie?"

"Yeah," the boy said. He'd been the one trying to wake her up.

"Yeah," the little girl echoed.

Sophie squinted again. It was so dark in the dank little room, without the small amount of light coming from under the door at the top of the steps, she might have worried she was blind. She forced herself to sit up, but the movement made her nauseous again. Great, she probably had a concussion. A quick hand to the back of her head came back wet and sticky. Blood.

"Who are you?"

"My name is Sophie. I'm with the FBI. Do you know what that means?"

"Nuh-uh," Katie said.

"I'm a police officer, and we've been looking for you." Sophie said. "Are either of you hurt?"

When she got negative responses from both of them she breathed a sigh of relief. Katie started to cry, and Sophie did her best to move closer. Her hand hit something on the floor that felt like the leg to a bed frame, and she reached up and found the thin mattress of a cot. A small hand grasped her fingers tight, and she fought back tears of her own.

"I want my mommy." Katie cried.

"I'm hungry," Timmy said softly.

"I know, kids. Other police officers are outside right now, trying to get us all away from the bad man who took you." Sophie hoped that was true. She could hear someone pacing above her. He was apparently on the phone, and even though she couldn't make out any of his words, she could definitely tell he wasn't very happy. Sophie reached for her cell phone, but of course it was gone. So was her gun. That didn't surprise her, but it pissed her off to feel so alone and helpless. Timmy moved to sit beside her and held her other hand. "We're going to get you both out of here. I promise."

A loud curse and then a crash came from upstairs. Sophie squeezed both kids' hands when she heard footsteps, and then the door at the top of the steps opened. She closed her eyes against the harsh bright white of a bulb overhead.

"Glad to see you decided to wake up and join us."

Sophie slowly opened her eyes and looked at the man for the first time. He didn't look like a killer. He looked like any regular guy you would see walking down the street. He was clearly nervous as hell though, which worried her. Shaking, he kept scratching his head as his eyes darted around to everything but her face. When someone's nerves were on edge he might do anything. He held her cell phone out to her.

"You'd better call your boss and let her know you're alive. I'm not sure she believed me, and I sure as hell don't want them busting in here." Marcus sat on the edge of the cot by Katie's feet and wiped his palms on his pants. The child pressed herself to the wall and pulled her feet under her. "This place is teeming with cops. I can't believe I managed to get myself into all this trouble."

He looked like he was about to cry. Sophie tried to come up with ways to calm him and kept looking at the gun he held—her gun. The safety was still engaged, and she gave a silent cheer for small victories. She turned the phone on but kept her attention on him.

"We want to help you, Marcus. Tell us who you're working for."

He looked at her and let out a humorless laugh.

"Do they teach you to say that in your cop training or something?"

Sophie didn't know what he was talking about and stared at him blankly.

"It's the same thing she said to me earlier."

"Who?"

He mimicked her. *"Olivia Andrews, FBI."*

Sophie's heart skipped a beat. She *was* out there.

"Nobody can help me, Agent Kane. No way am I getting out of here alive. You know that as well as I do."

"I *don't* know that, Marcus." Shit. If he thought he was doomed, that didn't look good for either her or the children. If he was going to die, then why bother letting them go? She had to make him believe she could help him. "If you're working for someone—doing these things on someone else's orders, under some kind of duress, we can help you. All you have to do is give us a name."

She held her breath while he seemed to consider her words. Tapping the gun's muzzle on his knee, he closed his eyes and tilted his head back. Sophie considered making a move to wrestle the gun away from him, but she was in no shape to move that fast. Just going the short distance from where she'd woken up to the cot had exhausted her and made the room spin. She turned so her back was against the wall next to the head of the cot and she was facing him, hoping to show through her actions that she wasn't a threat. A small hand touched her shoulder and she covered it with her own, squeezing gently to try to reassure Katie.

"I can't do that," Marcus said after a moment. "Not only because you wouldn't believe me, but if I do somehow manage to get out of here, he'll find me. He'll kill me *and* my mother. I can't let that happen to her because she's always done everything for me."

"You might be surprised by what I'd believe," Sophie told him, thinking back to Liv's theory about Mansfield. Could it be true?

He stood and headed back to the stairs before apparently remembering he had given Sophie her phone. He returned to the cot and sat back down while motioning for her to make a call.

"You have two minutes. Just let her know you're alive." He made a show of disengaging the gun's safety and pointing the muzzle at her face. His hand shook, but that didn't mean the bullet wouldn't hit home if he pulled the trigger.

Sophie's hands were shaking too while she pushed the buttons to make the call. She met Marcus's eyes over the barrel of the gun.

❖

"Everybody's in place, Boss," Gabe said when he met Liv at the van where their surveillance equipment was set up. They'd placed cameras in trees, hoping to figure out where in the house he was and where he might be holding Sophie, Timmy, and Katie. "There's nowhere for him to go. He's trapped."

"And I'm sure he knows that, Gabe." She tightened her Kevlar vest and checked for the fifth time that her gun was loaded. What she was about to do was risky, and no doubt Hal would tell her it was stupid. But he wasn't there yet, and she had to get the hostages out. She was hoping Sophie had learned enough in her brief training to keep Marcus calm.

"I wish you'd rethink this, Liv," Justin said from behind her. She turned to stare at him. "It's a dicey situation, and you shouldn't put yourself at risk to save someone else."

"She's a part of our team, Ingram," Liv said. He flinched but Liv never faltered. The only time she called him by his last name was when she was pissed. She knew he was well aware he couldn't change her mind. "I will not leave her in there to go through this alone. I have to at least try."

"Whatever you say." Justin turned and walked away. Liv felt bad for a split second, but she had more pressing matters than soothing Justin's ego.

She pulled her phone out to make a call to Marcus, but when she had it in her hand, it began to vibrate. Maybe he wanted to make his own deal.

"Andrews," she said into the phone.

"Liv, it's Sophie."

Liv's knees almost gave out. She would have fallen to the ground if Gabe hadn't grabbed her elbow to steady her. He looked at her with concern, but she shook her head and moved to the other side of the van.

"Thank God," she muttered. "Are you all right? Are Timmy and Katie in there too?"

"I'm fine, Liv. So are the children."

"I will get you out of there, Sophie," she said, and angrily wiped a tear from her cheek. If they somehow managed to get Sophie out of there alive she'd take a chance and see where this thing between them might lead. Maybe love and a relationship weren't really out of her realm of possibilities like she'd always thought.

"It's okay, Olivia." Sophie sounded like it was anything but okay, and Liv's heart hurt for her—for whatever she was dealing with. "I need to hang up now. I'll see you soon."

Liv stared at the phone in her hand and didn't try to stop the tears. She'd known Sophie for all of a month and was certain she cared more about Sophie Kane than she did the job. And she would probably never have the opportunity to tell her that.

CHAPTER TWENTY-FIVE

L iv couldn't stop the cry of anguish that escaped her when the call ended, and Justin was there by her side almost immediately. She was about to throw a punch into the side of the van when he grabbed her arm and held on tight.

"Get hold of yourself, Liv," he said with a quiet authority.

She met his eyes briefly, but all she could think about was Sophie being held hostage and Victor Nathan with a bullet hole in his head. Without a word, she pressed a button on her phone and held it to her ear while she listened to it ring. She hated calling Marcus Kraft using Sophie's number, but it was the only way she knew how to communicate with him.

"Agent Andrews, how nice to hear from you again," he said when he finally answered. "Are you ready to negotiate?"

"The only negotiation I'm doing is this," Liv said as she turned her head away from the disappointment in Justin's gaze. "I'm offering myself up in exchange for Agent Kane and the kids. Nothing else will be discussed until we make that swap."

She waited with growing impatience as he apparently thought about the deal. She paced as she kept glancing at the house.

"Why should I agree to that?" he finally asked.

"Because if you don't you won't make it out of that house alive." She looked up into the trees surrounding the building to make sure the snipers were all in place. They'd had to work fast to get everything set up, and for once things seemed to be going her way.

Two sharpshooters had their sights trained on the front door, and two more were in the back. She wasn't sure if they'd do any good, though, with all the trees and shrubbery around the house. She'd placed one on each side of the house in case he tried to escape out a window. No way would he be leaving the house alive no matter what he did, but she wasn't about to tell him that. "You have five minutes to make a decision. After that, all bets are off."

She disconnected the call and replaced the phone in her pocket. Justin came to her side when she motioned for him, and she put an arm around his shoulders.

"I don't like it, Liv," he said.

"Your opinion is duly noted, Ingram." She kept her eyes on the front door while she spoke. "If he agrees, I need you to promise me you'll get Sophie and those kids to safety immediately. He won't come out with them, and I'm sure he realizes we have sharpshooters out here, so he won't make himself visible from any of the windows. That means he could have a gun on them the whole time and we wouldn't know it. *Do not* stop until they're safely behind one of these cars or some trees. Do you understand me?"

"Yes," he said through gritted teeth. "Please don't take this the wrong way, but is she worth your life, Liv?"

"I'm going to pretend you didn't just ask me that. Don't you know I'd do it for you too? For any of you?" Liv tried to sound authoritative but knew she fell short. Yes, she'd do the same for any one of her team. They were family. Sophie wasn't a permanent part of their unit, but that didn't matter.

"I need to use the bathroom," Sophie said when Marcus hung up with Liv. If she'd foreseen being in this position she wouldn't have had so much coffee in her attempts to stay awake the night before. She cringed when he became agitated.

"Why would she want to trade places with you?" he asked, ignoring her request. "I don't understand why anyone would willingly do that."

He headed for the stairs, and just before he got there he turned around and stared at her. A brief moment of clarity, of utter desperation, in his expression let her know he had nothing to lose. He waved the gun at her, and she would have backed away to the far wall if she'd been physically able to.

"Unless there's something more than a job between the two of you." He smiled. His own cell phone began to ring, but he ignored it and instead walked back to her. "Is that it? Are the two of you involved?"

"No," Sophie answered, hoping she sounded suitably appalled. She was determined he wouldn't discover anything about her, especially her feelings for Liv. It pissed her off to think Liv would even suggest such an exchange. The phone stopped ringing but immediately started again. He looked exasperated as he put it to his ear.

"What?" he growled into the phone, and his expression went from angry to nervous in mere seconds. He turned away from her and spoke so quietly she couldn't hear what he was saying.

"Sophie?" Katie whispered.

She turned her head to look at the little girl. "What is it, sweetie?"

"I'm scared," she said, obviously trying very hard not to cry. Sophie noticed the ragged Teddy bear clutched to her chest.

Sophie forced herself to ignore the blinding pain in her head caused by moving and got up off the floor so she could sit next to her on the cot. Katie immediately let go of the bear and crawled into her lap. Her arms went around Sophie's neck, her head pressed tight against Sophie's shoulder. Timmy pushed himself against Sophie's side, looking as if he were trying very hard to be brave. She gave him a smile she hoped was reassuring.

"We'll be out of here soon, and I bet your mommy and daddy will be really happy to see you again." Sophie rocked back and forth slowly, praying she was telling the truth. Kraft seemed to forget he had company in the room with him and began to talk louder as his anxiety level escalated.

"Jesus, I didn't have a choice," he said, his back still to them. He turned suddenly and gave Sophie a long, considering look. He pulled the phone away from his ear and pushed the button to put the call on speaker. "She was snooping around the house."

"Why didn't you just kill her, Marcus? That would have solved all your problems. Now you've got so many cops outside your house you'll never get out of there alive."

Sophie looked at Marcus's face and saw his silent plea for her to understand. It dawned on her she was hearing Sergeant Mansfield's voice.

"You know I hate doing that. Was it you who killed that FBI agent?" Marcus asked him. He held Sophie's gaze while they both waited for him to answer. "Because I know they're going to try to pin that on me too."

"Yes, I did it. I'm just sorry it wasn't that bitch Andrews. You were stupid enough to take the damn kid with you to meet your cousin, and then you didn't even kill him like you were supposed to. You asked for a distraction so you could meet with him, Marcus, and I gave it to you. The agent saw the kid in your car when he came back out of the diner, and I got to him before he could call it in. If you give up my name, your entire family will pay, do you understand me?"

"You said yourself there're cops all over the place here, Mansfield. I have to give myself up. I don't have a choice."

"No!" he yelled. "You will not give up without a fight, Kraft. If you lead them to me, your mother will pay for it with her life."

Marcus finally looked away from Sophie before taking the call off speaker and turning away again.

Her heart thundered against her ribs.

She hadn't wanted to believe it, but Liv was right. Certain things suddenly made sense. Mansfield hadn't wanted them involved in the York abduction from the beginning. It had seemed an odd coincidence when he pulled the tail they had on Richard Kraft the very day Victor was killed, but obviously he'd been trying to protect Marcus—no, it was clear he didn't give a damn about Marcus. He was trying to protect himself. The questions were flying through her mind, and she had to actually remind herself to breathe again before she passed out.

She was trying to figure out a way to get her cell phone back when he ended his call and turned back to her. Her heart was beating so fast she could hardly concentrate.

"Sergeant Mansfield?" she managed to choke out. "Is that who's forcing you to do these things? Please, Marcus, let us help you. How did he not know you had him on speaker?"

"Does it matter? I'm a dead man whether he knew or not. I signed my own death warrant the second I borrowed money from him." The sheer panic was evident in his eyes. While Mansfield had been talking, the determined look in Marcus's eyes told her that he wanted to hand Mansfield over to them. Now that the conversation was over, he seemed to be having second thoughts. He sat on the bottom step and put his hands on each side of his head, the gun still in his right hand. "If I tell you everything you have to promise me you'll protect my mother."

"I swear we will, Marcus," she said. A light at the end of tunnel, so to speak? Did he really mean to let her out of there alive? "Tell me everything."

Before he could start talking, her cell rang again. He picked it up and answered quickly.

"I need a few more minutes," he said quietly, his voice a little too calm for Sophie's liking.

"I don't have a few more minutes, Marcus," Sophie could hear Liv saying.

"Please. Just ten more minutes, and I'll make the exchange, all right?" He glanced at Sophie. If he got the time she would know everything about the kidnappings and Mansfield's involvement in them. "Ten minutes, but you need to come down the driveway alone and unarmed. I'm not stupid enough to let you walk into my house with a weapon. And if I see anybody close to you, I'll kill all of my hostages, do you understand?"

"Let me talk to Agent Kane."

"Liv, please don't do this," Sophie begged as she put the phone to her ear. She watched Marcus's face as she spoke, and the serenity overtaking his expression scared her. He should have been nervous as hell right then, but he looked to be a man who'd come to peace with his fate. "It really doesn't feel right to me."

"I'll be fine, Sophie, but I need you to be honest with me. Are you hurt?"

"I may have a concussion, and my head is bleeding, but I'll be all right."

"Why does he want another ten minutes?"

"I think he's going to tell me the whole story." Sophie looked at him questioningly, relieved when he nodded. "You were right though. Mansfield is the one giving him his orders. It's okay, Liv. Ten minutes."

"Fine. He has them. Then I better see you and those kids walking out of there under your own power. Give the phone back to him."

Sophie sat in silence as Marcus spoke to Liv again. When he hung up, he took a deep breath and sat at the foot of the cot facing her. He looked at Katie and smiled.

"I'm so sorry for what I did—taking you away from your mother. I'm not going to hurt you though, okay?"

Katie nodded and hugged Sophie tighter, her head turned away from Marcus. He met Sophie's eyes then. "I won't hurt you or Timmy either. I panicked when I found you outside. I'm sorry. I know I told your boss I'd kill you, but I won't. I just need to have some kind of control over this whole mess."

"It's okay, Marcus. I understand you did what you had to do. Your survival instincts were kicking in." Sophie held his gaze and he seemed to relax a bit. She wished she'd had more than three days of hostage-negotiating training before being thrown into such a volatile situation. He was talking though, and she hoped she could keep him wanting to open up. "I also know you've only been abducting children because you were forced to. I just need you to tell me why he was forcing you, and what he's doing with the children. We can help you, Marcus. I promise."

"I doubt that, but it was a nice try." He attempted to smile, or at least that was how it looked to her, but he closed his eyes briefly before going on. "I used to drive to Atlantic City. A lot. I would spend my entire paycheck on the blackjack tables. My mother finally forced me to go to Gamblers Anonymous, and it helped for a while."

Sophie studied his profile when he turned his head and looked up at the lone window. She fought the urge to prompt him, her instincts telling her he needed to do it on his own terms. She bit her tongue and waited for him to continue.

"But then they started opening casinos in Pennsylvania. At first it wasn't so bad because they didn't have any table games, and I never liked the slots much. When they finally started the table games though, I got in way too deep. The Sands Casino in Bethlehem quickly became my favorite place, and I was there almost every night. I couldn't seem to make myself stop, no matter how hard I tried. One night after I ran out of money, I met a guy there who knew someone that could get me a large amount of cash fast, and I jumped at the chance. After a couple of weeks, when I couldn't make my first payment, they threatened me and my mother."

"How much money are we talking about, Marcus?"

"A hundred grand."

How could anyone lose that much money at a casino? It seemed unfathomable. He was quiet then, and Sophie was almost positive she saw a tear run down his cheek, but he turned his head back to look at her as he wiped it away. He forced a smile.

"Who was the guy you spoke with about the money? Did he seek you out, or did you find him? Everything you tell me is going to be used to put Mansfield away for a very long time."

"I don't remember the guy's name. He approached me one night after I hit my daily limit at the ATM machine. I think he was probably just there to find people like me for Mansfield to recruit. I'm not the only one doing this." He pointed to Katie and Timmy, and Sophie nodded in understanding as his words took hold.

"I honestly don't know if Mansfield is the head honcho, or if he's working on someone else's orders. He's the only one I've ever dealt with."

"What do they do with the kids?" Sophie wasn't sure she wanted the answer, and she held Katie tighter, covering her ears as much as she could without being obvious. A quick glance at Timmy assured her he wasn't interested in what they were talking about. He was pulling at threads in his jeans and humming softly to himself.

"I don't know," he said, with a glance at Katie. "But they didn't want the ones who had disabilities. I wanted to just let them go, but I couldn't. Mansfield ordered me to kill them because he said they could lead the authorities to me, and he didn't trust me not to give him up."

"Then why is he still alive, Marcus?" She didn't want to attract Timmy's attention, and she knew Marcus understood what she was asking by the way he glanced at the boy.

"I can't do it anymore," he said quietly. He met her eyes and tears welled up, threatening to spill over. "You wouldn't believe how much blood there is. I killed the girl with autism, and that boy who had Asperger's. They were the last two I took before him. I'd rather die than have to murder another child."

Sophie nodded, cringing inside. He'd killed two children, and he was desperate. As much as he said he didn't want to do it again, desperate men did desperate things. She decided to keep him talking.

"Do you have other proof that Mansfield was behind everything? I mean something tangible that would link him to it all? I can certainly testify to hearing his voice on the phone, but…"

"He's a cop, so they'll probably be more inclined to believe him than me." He shrugged and looked down at his feet. "That's why I'm letting you out of here. You can make them believe you, right? I swear I'm not going to hurt you. But you need to make sure he doesn't get to my mother."

"I'm afraid we'll need more than my testimony about what he said during what he thought was a private phone conversation with you."

"I have a couple of e-mails on my laptop. It's upstairs in my bedroom. You have people who can figure out where they came from, right?"

"Yes, we do. Anything else?"

"I have his home and mobile numbers programmed on here." He pulled his cell out of his pocket and looked at it. "And a couple of voice mails that I saved. In one of them he's pretty pissed because I hadn't gotten rid of Timmy yet. But the best part? He bought this house to put me up in. I'm sure you'll find his name attached to it if you investigate."

"That's good, Marcus." She doubted Mansfield would have been stupid enough to use his own name or to even make the purchase himself, but in her experience, even the smartest criminals made the stupidest mistakes. And these certainly weren't the smartest criminals. "We can use all of those things to help you."

CHAPTER TWENTY-SIX

"Gabe!" Liv called when she hung up with Sophie. He ran to her, and she put her arm around his shoulder. "Kane got confirmation that Mansfield's behind it all. We have an APB out on him, right?"

"It went out before we even got to his house this morning."

"Good man." She squeezed his shoulder briefly, trying not to let on how nervous she was about the exchange. "Promise me something."

"What?"

"If everything goes to hell here, you'll get Sophie and those kids out of here in one piece." She'd already asked Justin, but it couldn't hurt to have more than one person ready to whisk Sophie out of harm's way, could it?

"You'll be able to do that yourself."

"Gabe," she said, with a shake of her head.

"Hey, Liv, it's all going to be over by tonight," Gabe told her, and ran his hand over his face. "We're going to close this case, and we'll all be home in time for Vic's funeral next week. Promise *me* you'll be there."

She smiled and nodded before releasing him. Taking a deep breath, she was trying to ready herself for what she was going to do when Justin ran up beside her.

"Hal's less than five minutes away. Please, at least wait until he gets here to do this."

"I can't." The front door was opening slowly and she steeled herself. "I need to get them out of there now."

❖

"Come out with us," Sophie said as Marcus led them up the stairs to the kitchen. "Turn yourself in. Please. You have some good evidence against Mansfield."

"I know you have snipers out there just waiting for me to show my face." He took her by the arm and walked toward the front door. "Your boss is the only one who can help me now."

Sophie looked at him quizzically, but his expression was unreadable. She took note of the curtains drawn on every window. He stopped but pointed toward the door for them to continue. He gave her back her cell phone and handed her his as well, which perplexed her even more.

"Take this. My pin for retrieving messages is 3266. I'm happy you believe me, but I don't want it to get into the wrong hands. Some of these cops could be working for him." He placed her gun in his waistband, apparently not trusting her quite so far as to give it back to her. "Go now, before they start thinking I'm backing out on the exchange."

"Marcus, please don't do this," she said, beginning to panic. She realized what his intentions were and was powerless to stop him. "It doesn't have to be this way. Nobody else has to die."

"Get the hell out of here now before I change my mind about letting you walk away at all," he said, more calmly than she would have imagined possible. He had come to grips with his decision, and for him it was the only way out of an impossible situation. To emphasize his point, he grabbed a semi-automatic pistol from the table in the hall and pointed it at Katie, never taking his eyes from Sophie's. "Now."

She picked Katie up and carried her through the front door. Timmy walked beside her, gripping her hand. She heard Liv yell for everyone to hold their fire, and then she was walking slowly toward them. Sophie fought the urge to run to her. It would only make the pain in her head worse, and some cops were trigger-happy. If they thought she posed a threat, Liv's order to stand down wouldn't mean a thing to them.

"Are you okay?" Liv called to her.

"Liv, get down!" Sophie yelled as she held Katie tighter against her body and yanked Timmy in front of her to shield him. She heard a noise behind her when she was only a few steps away and turned to see Marcus a few steps inside the doorway, the semi-automatic pointed toward them. She immediately fell to the ground and did her best to cover the children's bodies with her own even as she yelled at Liv to get down.

Liv walked toward them and watched in confusion when Sophie dropped and curled herself around the sobbing kids. Sophie was yelling something at her, but she couldn't comprehend what it was. The three of them had come out before she made it to the house for the exchange. Something was wrong. But she couldn't look away from Sophie. There was blood. So much damn blood on Sophie's shirt and the side of her face. The desire to kill the bastard overwhelmed her. She looked at the house then and saw the gun pointed directly at her, but he was far enough away from the doorway, still in the shadows, that the snipers wouldn't see the threat right away. She wished she hadn't told her team to stay back. She threw her hands up and shook her head quickly.

"You don't have to do this, Marcus," she said, hoping her actions and her words would clue the cops around her in on what was about to happen.

"I can't go back to jail," he yelled back. "I'd never survive it."

She heard two shots in rapid succession, and almost instantly pain seared her left shoulder, just below the collarbone, and her leg. She fell to the ground in stunned agony and heard Sophie cry out. She was dimly aware of a cacophony of gunfire then, and everyone was shouting as she turned her head slowly toward Sophie before the red haze clouding her vision faded to black.

❖

Sophie wanted nothing more than to run to Liv's aid, but she'd be risking her own life as well as the children's if she moved in the midst of a gunfight. They were stuck between Kraft and the police, and she curled tighter around the screaming children, panic welling up uncontrollably. Damn it, she saw it coming, but it was too late for her to stop it. His calmness while she'd talked to Liv on the phone the last time. The remark he made about her boss being the only one that could help him. She cursed herself for not paying attention to the signs. She should have seen it earlier than she did, and now Liv could be dead because of her.

She turned her head so she could look at Liv, who lay on her back, her eyes open and staring right at Sophie.

Liv reached out to her just before her eyes slid shut and her body went slack. Sophie tried not to look at the blood spreading in the dirt next to Liv's leg as she grabbed her hand.

"No, damn it!" Blood pumped out of Liv's leg with every beat of her heart. She was alive, but apparently an artery had been hit, and it wouldn't take long for her to bleed out.

It seemed like hours before the deafening noise finally ceased, then Frank was at her side, urging her to let go of Katie so he could get her to the waiting ambulance. Gabe pried Timmy's hands from Sophie's waistband and ran with him to the ambulance. Relieved of the children, she scrambled on her hands and knees to Liv's side. Placing one hand firmly on the inside of Liv's thigh she pressed as hard as she could to try to slow the blood loss.

"Is she alive?" Justin asked as he dropped to his knees beside her, even as he frantically waved the paramedics over. The look on Justin's face was a mixture of grief and anger.

"Yes." Sophie pressed harder, her tears mixing with the blood pooling beneath her hands.

The medics pushed them aside, but Sophie refused to go far. Justin put his arm around her, and she melted into him, immediately putting her arms around his waist. Neither of them seemed to notice that Sophie was covered in blood. She felt immense relief when the medic ripped Liv's shirt open to reveal the Kevlar vest. The point of impact was obvious, and Liv would have a hell of a bruise, but the bullet hadn't made it to her skin. Sophie's attention was drawn again to the wound in Liv's right thigh, where another medic was applying pressure and yelling orders to his partner. She spared a brief glance at the man who had shot Liv, his lifeless body sprawled on the porch, blood spattered all over the walls behind him. She shuddered and leaned into Justin.

Liv's blood was everywhere, soaking rapidly through the towels they pressed to her leg. She was unconscious. The medics were working frantically to stop the bleeding while they got her on a gurney.

"Will she make it?" Justin asked the question Sophie couldn't quite bring herself to pose.

"Her pressure's dropping fast, and she's lost a lot of blood. We're taking her to Easton Hospital. She'll be in good hands."

"That doesn't really answer the question though, does it?" Justin muttered to their retreating backs. He tightened his hold on Sophie, and she was grateful for his strength. "You should go with her, Kane. You need to be checked out too."

"No, you go so she's not alone," Sophie said, even though every part of her wanted to do what he suggested. They still had a criminal to catch, and she needed to see that through. Liv would want her to finish what they'd started, not sit in a waiting room while Mansfield got away. As Hal ran up to them, she showed him the cell phone Kraft had given her. "Kraft's phone. We need to get information off it. Mansfield's on it giving orders."

"You need to get checked out, Kane," he said as he took the phone from her. "You're covered in blood."

"No, I need to help retrieve the information from the phone. Justin's going with Liv." Sophie knew her tone indicated her resolve to stay and help. She hoped Hal wouldn't fight her on the decision. She breathed a sigh of relief when he finally nodded once before turning toward Kraft's lifeless body, where the rest of the team had gone after getting the children to safety.

"Gabe!" Hal yelled. When Gabe looked up he motioned him over. "You and Frank stay here and take care of things. Make sure you go over the house with a fine-tooth comb. We need to get physical proof Mansfield was giving him his orders. Justin's going with Liv in the ambulance. I'm taking Sophie to the van so we can retrieve information from Kraft's phone."

"No problem, Boss," Gabe said, then stopped short, looking at Sophie as though he knew what she was feeling about him calling Hal "Boss," even though he was. He started to walk away but stopped and turned back, his gaze on Sophie's face. "Is Liv going to be all right?"

"I don't know," Justin said as he ran toward the ambulance. Sophie almost started to cry at his desperate tone, but she bit her bottom lip and turned away from them. When Gabe went back to work, Hal took Sophie's arm and led her away from the scene.

❖

"You really need to get to the hospital, Kane," Hal said about twenty minutes after they got into the van and started extracting the information from Kraft's cell phone. Sophie had filled him in on everything she'd heard and what Kraft told her about Mansfield. Gabe confirmed Kraft's story about the e-mails from Mansfield on the laptop, and as soon as they'd listened to Mansfield's voice mails on the phone, they put word out to all the law-enforcement agencies in Pennsylvania, New Jersey, and New York.

Justin had called to let them know Liv was in serious condition, and they were taking her in for surgery to remove the bullet from her leg. Sophie clung to the fact that Liv was alive and tried not to think about all the things that could go wrong during surgery.

A paramedic had tried to convince Sophie she needed to go to the hospital for stitches in her head, but she refused. He'd bandaged her as well as he could and let her go, but made sure it was known she was going against his advice. Now, sitting there in the van, she honestly couldn't fight anymore. The adrenaline rush was wearing off fast, and the pain in her head was so excruciating she just wanted to sleep. She also wanted to be there when they brought Mansfield in, but since they had no idea where he was, she knew she was being unreasonable. With fresh blood running down her neck, she wouldn't last much longer without medical care.

"I'm taking you now whether you want to go or not," Hal said. He grabbed his keys and came to her side as her eyes slid closed. "Kane, stay with me, damn it."

She felt him shake her arm gently, but she couldn't find the strength to respond. She heard him somewhere in the distance yelling for someone to call for an ambulance, and then there was nothing.

CHAPTER TWENTY-SEVEN

Incessant beeping infiltrated Liv's mind as she fought her way back to consciousness. She wished someone would make it stop. Other than that irritating noise, everything was completely silent. She had something in her right hand, but couldn't figure out what. Her eyes felt like gritty cement but she managed to crack them open. She squinted down at her left hand and saw the IV line, and it dawned on her she was in a darkened hospital room. Memories flooded back.

Sophie. Sophie had been literally in the middle of the firefight at Marcus Kraft's residence. Liv couldn't concentrate on anything but the need to find out if Sophie was okay. She struggled to sit up and fell back with a groan.

"Fuck." She closed her eyes again when she attempted to take a deep breath and was rewarded with a sharp pain in her left shoulder. The pain in her leg was possibly even worse than the one in her shoulder. Someone squeezed her right hand, and she slowly turned her head to meet crystal-blue eyes filled with tears. "Mom?"

"Thank God you're awake, Olivia," Janet Andrews said. She brushed Liv's hair away from her eyes. "Do you remember what happened, honey?"

"I was shot," Liv answered with a grimace, trying to find a comfortable position for her leg.

"Twice," her father said from her other side.

Kyle Andrews had been a handsome young man when Liv first met him, and at fifty-seven, he was still as dashing as ever, even with the gray hair at his temples. Both of them had aged gracefully, and Liv wished for a moment that she'd inherited their genes.

"Your mother almost had a stroke when she got the phone call."

"Kyle, stop joking," Janet said, but something in her eyes said it wasn't far from the truth.

"Where's Sophie?" Liv asked, ignoring their playful banter. She looked from her mother to her father, but neither of them answered right away. "Is she okay? What about the kids?"

"Calm down, Olivia," her father said, a gentle hand on her arm. "Sophie's fine. She's here in the hospital being treated for a minor concussion and a nasty gash in the back of her head. They were worried about infection, but she's stable now. Both of the children have been checked for injuries and were released to go home with their parents."

Liv breathed a sigh of relief and closed her eyes. Being able to get those kids back to their parents was what the job was all about. Thanks to Sophie they were able to do it.

"You need to rest," her mother said, and placed her lips against Liv's forehead. "I was worried about you, honey. You lost a lot of blood."

"How long have I been here?"

"About twenty-four hours," said a man in a lab coat, who joined them. "The bullet to your leg nicked your femoral artery, which is why you bled so much. The paramedics did a hell of a job getting you stabilized before you ever arrived here. And you're going to have a nasty bruise below your shoulder. You're a very lucky woman. Without your vest, that shot would have gone awfully close to your heart."

"I need to see Sophie," Liv said. She struggled to sit up, but the three of them successfully stopped her from moving too much. It confused her to be more concerned about Sophie than herself. She'd never felt that way before about anyone. If she'd learned anything in the few weeks she'd known Sophie, though, it was to not question her feelings. "Please."

"Sophie Kane?" the doctor asked, and Liv nodded. "I'll see if she's okay to leave her bed. I know she's been pestering the staff to let her see you."

He used her bedside phone to call the nurses' station to have them bring Sophie to her room. Liv felt inordinately happy to hear that Sophie was just as anxious to see her. She forced herself to lie there patiently while he examined her wounds before he left. When he was gone, she looked at her father.

"It's nice to see you guys, but I wish it were under better circumstances," she said.

"You're going to be okay. I'd say that's damn good circumstances," he replied with a smile. "Justin's waiting outside to see you. He's been pretty eager for you to wake up. I think he has some news."

Liv nodded and closed her eyes while he walked out to get Justin. She felt safe here with her mother holding her hand.

"Is Sophie someone I should know about?" her mother asked quietly.

Liv turned her head to look at her and couldn't stop the smile that tugged at her lips.

"I don't know. It's something she and I need to talk about." Liv watched her mother's expression turn hopeful and squeezed her hand. "I hope so."

"So do I, Liv," she said. "I so want you to be happy. I've told you before, but I couldn't love you any more if I'd given birth to you myself. You're a wonderful woman, and you deserve to find the happiness your father and I have."

Liv closed her eyes to prevent the tears that would come if she held her mother's gaze too long. She remembered telling them when she graduated from Quantico that she wanted to lose herself in her job because she was certain she would never find something as perfect as what they had.

"I want that too," she whispered just as the door opened and Justin followed her father in. When she looked at Justin, she could see he was about to burst with some news. She couldn't help but smile at his exuberance.

"We'll leave you two alone for a few minutes," her father said, motioning toward the door. "Come on, Janet." He pointed at Justin. "Not too long though, hear? Don't get her all worked up."

Justin nodded and waited for them to leave before he turned back to Liv. She almost laughed at how he was trying to hold everything in. She hadn't seen him smile like that in months.

"I know you're dying to tell me something, so spit it out, man."

"Marcus Kraft is dead, which I assume was his plan all along. He told Sophie everything before he sent her out the door. He gave her his cell phone and the pin number to get his voice mails, which is why we think he intended to commit suicide-by-cop. He wouldn't have given her the information if he'd thought he was going to make it out of there. He knew shooting at you would accomplish his goal." Justin sat in the chair her mother had vacated and propped his elbows on the bed. He still looked like the proverbial cat that ate the canary.

Liv tried and failed to wait patiently for him to go on. "Are you going to tell me whether or not you found Mansfield?" Despite her annoyance with his drawn-out way of telling a story, her pulse quickened in anticipation. "I'm in pain here, Justin."

"He was picked up early this morning in Lancaster County. We discovered he had a sister in Ohio, so we figured he was heading that way." Justin sat back in his chair and Liv closed her eyes, feeling a great sense of relief. "They brought him back to Allentown this afternoon, along with his plane ticket out of the country. Hal is pretty fucking impressed you had it all figured out before anyone else did. The entire team is. I love it when you follow a gut feeling, Liv."

"But we never would have known for sure if Kane hadn't disobeyed my orders," Liv pointed out with a wry grin. She turned her head away and watched the door, hoping Sophie would walk in any second. She deserved to hear all of it too. "Was he working for someone?"

"Not as far as we can tell. Your father said Sophie was coming to see you. I'll wait to tell you the rest when she's here too."

Not thirty seconds later the door opened again and a nurse pushed Sophie's wheelchair into the room. She situated it next to the bed, and again relief washed over Liv when Sophie took her hand.

"Are you really all right?" she asked quietly.

"That's what the doctor says." Liv smiled warmly at her. Why in God's name had she ever tried to fight the things she was feeling for Sophie? Even disheveled and wearing a hospital gown with a blanket over her legs, she was still the most beautiful woman Liv had ever seen.

"Ten minutes, then you need to go back to your room, Miss Kane," the nurse said in a tone that left no room for negotiation. They were silent until the woman left, then Liv gently squeezed the hand lying in hers.

"How's your head?"

"Fine. I'm going home tomorrow."

"I wish I was. I hate hospitals."

"Hello," Justin said from the other side of the bed. "Just wanted to make sure you guys knew I was still here."

"Did he tell you?" Sophie asked. Liv liked the way Sophie's thumb was gently caressing the back of her hand. It soothed her.

"Part of it. He was making me wait for you to get here before he'd give up the rest of it." Liv looked at him and raised her eyebrows, urging him to finish his story.

"I knew something was going on between you two," Justin said with a grin.

"Nothing's going on, Ingram," Liv said, a bit too gruffly. Sophie pulled her hand away and Liv hated her pained expression. Why couldn't she stop to think about what she said before it left her mouth? She wanted to apologize, but she needed to get whatever information Justin had for them first, and what she had with Sophie felt too new, too fragile, to open up to interrogation, even by her closest friend. She'd kick his ass out of the room when he finished telling, and then she could tell Sophie she hadn't meant what she said. Justin looked between the two of them as though he didn't believe what she was saying, but he finally shrugged.

"It appears Mansfield really is the top dog here. He had other people working with and for him, but as far as we've been able to tell, he controlled it all and was using people's addictions— gambling, drugs, whatever—to get them to do what he wanted.

We've arrested about five other people in connection with this too. From the evidence we've gathered—and his signed confession, if you can believe that—the kidnappings appear to have started around the same time his daughter and her husband adopted a little girl."

"So he did all of it so he could sell kids for adoption?" Liv asked, sending a silent thank you to whoever was responsible for making the reason for it all so simple.

"Yep, and he kept records. We know where all the kids went, and it will take some time, but they should all eventually be returned to their families. No big crime ring, no black market to other countries. Just a greedy bastard who realized from his own daughter's struggles that he could make money from selling kids to couples who really wanted them." He gave Sophie a pointed look across the bed. "You're the one who broke the case, Kane. Good work."

Sophie chuckled. "Who knew anything good would come from my stupidity?"

"You aren't stupid, Sophie," Liv said quietly. "I probably would have done the same thing in your situation."

Sophie looked like she wanted to say something more, but then shook her head and looked away. Liv wished the circumstances were different, and she could be alone with Sophie, but the case was still the most important element at the moment.

"So he started it to help his daughter. I guess the potential for profit was just too great for him to turn his back on it after that," Liv said, steering Justin back to the current topic. She'd have time to congratulate Sophie for a job well done later.

"Why did they kill the kids with disabilities?" Sophie asked.

"Honestly? Who wants to adopt a baby with a disability? Apparently these people were paying upwards of a hundred grand to adopt, and for that amount of money, you'd expect a healthy kid, right? That's what he was promising them, anyway."

"If Kraft hadn't told Sophie everything, we might never have caught Mansfield." Liv owed a lot more to Sophie than just congratulations. She wasn't sure she could ever thank her enough for everything she did. "Just because I had a theory he was involved didn't mean anything would have ever come from it."

"We probably would have gotten him anyway, because we had the e-mails and his phone records. Kraft made a lot of calls to Mansfield's cell, as well as his home and office numbers," Justin said. "But Sophie was certainly able to point us toward him a lot sooner."

"He actually confessed to everything?" Liv was skeptical. Mansfield didn't strike her as the type to give up without a fight.

"He denied it at first, but when he was faced with all the evidence against him, his lawyer advised him that confessing would probably be easier on him and his family." Justin was clearly still high on the adrenaline of breaking the case. Usually they were all happy beyond belief when a difficult case broke, and she'd be overjoyed too if she wasn't stuck in a hospital bed.

"The only downside is, in exchange for his full confession, they've agreed to sentence him in Northampton County rather than Lehigh."

"Too worried he'll run into someone he put away?" Liv asked sarcastically.

"He confessed to killing Victor too."

"He said that in the phone call Marcus let me listen in on," Sophie said. Liv looked at her, surprised. She didn't know Sophie had been privy to a phone conversation. Liv gave her a questioning glance, and she explained Marcus's actions before his death.

"Why would Mansfield give such a detailed description of what he did that morning?" Justin asked. "By all accounts, Marcus was a grunt being forced to do things he had no desire to do. It just strikes me as odd that Mansfield would give him that much information."

"It's a power trip, that's all," Liv said. She closed her eyes and rested her head on her pillow. "He wanted to boast about what he'd done, and he knew Kraft had zero chance of surviving. In his mind, he was getting away with it all, so why not brag? Classic villain syndrome."

"Richard Kraft is being charged with obstruction," Justin said.

"Good. If he'd cooperated with us from the beginning, maybe we could have gotten to his cousin before he kidnapped Katie," Sophie said. Liv looked at her, but Sophie refused to meet her eyes. "And Victor wouldn't have had to die."

"Time to go back to your room now," the nurse said as she walked in and headed straight for Sophie's wheelchair. Liv was certain the woman was back way before the allotted ten minutes had ended. She didn't want Sophie to leave yet.

"Will I see you again before you leave tomorrow?" Liv reached for Sophie's hand but the nurse pulled her out of reach.

"I don't know, Liv. Maybe it's not such a good idea," Sophie said, sounding tired. Liv just stared after them as they walked out of the room. She nodded at Justin when he decided to leave too, suddenly looking as wiped out as she felt.

Liv would have seriously considered going after Sophie, but she was exhausted. She felt like she could sleep for the next year. She'd have plenty of time to talk to Sophie later.

CHAPTER TWENTY-EIGHT

L iv was finally released from the hospital in three more days. Her parents objected, but she insisted they take her to Victor Nathan's funeral before she went home. The whole team was there, and Sophie too. Liv tried to catch her eye without being obvious, but Sophie never came near her and, worse yet in Liv's eyes, didn't even acknowledge her. Liv tried a couple of times to approach her, but with the cane her doctor insisted she use, Sophie had no problem keeping away from her, subtly putting distance between them every time Liv tried to get closer. Liv decided she could take a hint and asked her parents to take her home as soon as the service was over. Obviously Sophie had changed her mind, and it hurt—more than she thought a woman could possibly hurt her.

Her leg still felt like hell, and the bruise above her left breast would be with her for a long time, but she'd never been happier to walk into her own apartment. Of course she did so with her father's assistance, but she could deal with that.

"Kim has been anxious to see you, Liv," her mother said after she'd gotten her situated on the couch. "Do you think you'll be up to seeing her when she gets home from school?"

"Sure," Liv said distractedly. She closed her eyes to rest, but couldn't see anything but Sophie's face. That had been happening quite a bit in the past few days, and she chose to believe it was simply because Sophie had been ignoring her since that day in the hospital with Justin. She'd said something stupid, sure, but did she deserve to be completely ignored? Was it so bad Sophie couldn't forgive her? Or had she only imagined that Sophie shared her feelings in the first place?

"Kyle, why don't you go talk to Mary and let her know Kim can come over when she gets home."

"I'll be right back," he said before Liv heard the door opening and closing again.

"Olivia," her mother said quietly.

Liv chose to ignore her and feigned sleep. Apparently her mother knew her too well.

"Olivia, look at me."

Liv did as she was told. Her mother's eyes showed genuine concern, and Liv shook her head, but that didn't stop her mother.

"You haven't been yourself since Justin and Sophie left your room a few days ago," she said. She held onto Liv's hand as she spoke. "I'm worried about you."

"I was shot, Mom," Liv reminded her. "Don't you think I might have some kind of an adjustment period after something like that?"

"Don't try to bullshit me," Janet said with a sly grin. "You're upset because you haven't seen Sophie. Don't think I didn't notice the way she avoided you today, Olivia. She was the first person you asked about when you woke up, and now you're not speaking to one another. What's going on between you two?"

"Nothing." Liv closed her eyes again and sighed. "She expressed an interest and I told her I wouldn't get involved with a team member."

"But you did."

Liv looked at her again, wondering how mothers always knew when you weren't telling them the entire truth. She wanted more with Sophie than she'd ever wanted with Emily, or any other woman for that matter, and it scared her. Now that they weren't working together, she wasn't sure how to proceed. It seemed somehow desperate to call and invite her over, so she'd decided over the past couple of days to leave it up to Sophie.

"Yes, I did." Liv hated admitting that. It made her feel weak. Sophie broke through every defense she'd spent years perfecting, which disconcerted her.

"How long have you known her?"

Liv thought for a moment, recalling when Sophie had opened the door to the motel room looking incredibly beautiful.

"A little over a month."

"Well, you aren't going to be working for at least the next few weeks, so maybe you should spend some time getting to know her away from the job." Janet stood and went to the kitchen, then came back a moment later and handed Liv a glass of water and a pain pill. "Take this, and then you should sleep for a bit. When you wake up you can call her and ask her over for dinner."

Liv nodded and took the pill, wondering how the hell she could get out of that. With any luck, she'd sleep until Kim arrived, and maybe her mother would forget about it.

Liv couldn't believe her luck. Her mother *had* forgotten about making her call Sophie. She was settling in for a couple of hours to herself because her parents had taken Kim out to a movie. As she reached for the television remote someone knocked softly on the door. Not sure if she'd really heard it, she set the remote down without turning the TV on and listened. The knock came again, but louder. She struggled to get up with the cane, cursing under her breath all the way to the door. When she looked through the peephole, her heart stopped beating.

Sophie stood there looking around the hallway, and Liv was afraid she might actually run away if she didn't open the door soon, so she did. When Sophie looked at her and smiled shyly, Liv's heart swelled.

"Hi," Liv said, uncharacteristically nervous.

"Hi."

They stood there gazing at each other for a few moments, neither of them knowing what to say to break the ice. Sophie looked past Liv into her apartment. "Are you going to invite me in?"

"I'm sorry." Liv took a step back and motioned for her to enter. When she saw a small golden retriever puppy following her into the apartment, Liv hesitated. "What the hell is that?"

"A puppy. Don't tell me you've never seen one before," Sophie said with a grin.

"Very funny," Liv said under her breath. She followed Sophie into the living room, where she was apparently waiting to be invited to sit. "Have a seat. Can I get you something to drink?"

"I can get it, if you don't mind my snooping around your kitchen."

"Snoop away. Make yourself at home." Liv sat down and the puppy instantly jumped up on the couch next to her. She watched him in silence, and every time he looked at her his little tail started wagging. She smiled and scratched behind his ears. "Why is there a dog in my apartment, Kane?"

"Hal took him from Kraft's house," Sophie called back from the kitchen. "He gave two to Victor's family, and this one is yours if you want him. If you don't, I'll keep him."

At the sound of her voice in the other room, the puppy took off at a run to find her. Liv shook her head in amusement when she heard another knock at the door.

"Jesus, what's going on? I haven't had this many visitors at once in months."

"I can get it if you want me to," Sophie called from the kitchen.

"No. Don't worry." Liv got back to her feet and went to open the door. Regret at having not looked through the peephole washed over her when she saw Emily standing there. Emily's eyes went right to the cane in her hand before she walked into the apartment.

"Thank God, you're all right, Olivia," Em said, before stepping closer to kiss her.

Liv backed away and glanced toward the kitchen, which wasn't visible from the front door.

"What's wrong, baby?"

"Excuse me?" Liv asked incredulously. "What's wrong with *me*? What are you doing here, Emily? You broke up with me, remember?"

"Oh, please, I was mad." Emily walked farther into the apartment, as if she belonged there. At least she hadn't used her key to just barge in without knocking. "You know I don't mean the things I say when I'm mad."

"Apparently I don't know that, Em. Maybe *you* didn't mean what you said, but I did. You need to move on because I can't give you what you need." Liv felt the need to protect Sophie from Emily's wrath, so she went to the fireplace, which was directly opposite the kitchen. She knew Em would keep her focus on her and not look around. "I don't want to be with you anymore."

"Are you here alone?" Em asked, apparently not having heard what Liv said. "Don't you need someone to take care of you?"

Liv knew the look in Em's eyes. The kind of *taking care* of her Em had in mind usually occurred in the bedroom. Liv shook her head and was about to tell Em to get out when she heard Sophie speak.

"I assure you she's not here alone, and I'm perfectly capable of taking care of her."

Liv swallowed loudly at the possessive look on Sophie's face. Damn, Liv never would have thought jealousy would turn her on, but heat flooded her. Sophie looked like the sexiest woman in the world. Emily whipped around to see who was talking, and Liv cringed at the once-over Emily gave Sophie. Sophie stood her ground, resting casually against the wall, her arms crossed over her chest.

"Who the hell are you?" Emily asked.

"Special Agent Sophie Kane, FBI. And you are?"

"Not amused," Em said before turning back to Liv. "What's going on here?"

Liv hesitated for a moment as she thought back to her response to Justin when the same subject came up. She wasn't about to make that mistake again. She glanced at Sophie, who was looking at her as though she, too, wanted to hear her answer.

"I don't know, Em, but I'm hoping Sophie and I can figure it out together." Liv relaxed a bit when Sophie smiled at her and turned her full attention to Em. "And we certainly don't need you here to help us do that. I want my key back, and you need to leave."

Liv waited for Em's notorious temper to flare but was pleasantly surprised when she pulled her key ring out of her purse and removed the one to Liv's apartment before setting it on the coffee table.

"Call me when you get tired of her, because I know you will. You've never been the type to stay with one woman very long," she said, her smile full of malice. Liv almost bodily threw Emily out of the apartment. If she hadn't been injured, she would have done exactly that.

"Get out, Emily," Liv said. She did her best to escort her to the door. "And you're wrong about me. I just haven't met the woman who could keep me satisfied enough to *want* to stay with her very long."

Emily was outside the apartment by the time Liv had finished speaking, and when she turned around to say something no doubt hateful, Liv smiled and shut the door in her face.

CHAPTER TWENTY-NINE

P lease, sit down so we can talk."
Liv took Sophie's hand and led her to the couch. They sat a few feet apart, and Liv put her leg up on the coffee table to ease the pressure on it. The puppy took up residence between them, his butt against Liv's leg and his head resting on Sophie's thigh.

"You need to explain something to me," Liv said. "As soon as I told Justin nothing was going on between us I knew I'd made a mistake. It was a reflex. I didn't want anyone to know I have feelings for you, because of what happened the last time I got involved with another agent. I'm truly sorry. But then tonight, you heard me tell Emily there definitely *is* something going on, but you don't look totally happy with that. Why?"

"I'm scared," Sophie said quietly. She sat ramrod straight and looked at some point across the room she must have found interesting. Liv let out a frustrated sigh.

"Damn it, will you please look at me?" After another minute or two, Sophie finally turned her head. "Scared of what?"

"I've never felt this way about anyone before, Liv. What if Emily's right? What happens when you get tired of me?"

"That won't happen." Liv tentatively took Sophie's hand, feeling inordinately pleased when she didn't pull away.

"How can you be so sure?"

"Because I've never felt this way about anyone either."

Sophie gazed at the puppy between them, and Liv was content for a moment to simply watch her in silence. Eventually, though, her curious nature won out.

"How did you know where I live?"

"We brought Kim home after the ball game that night."

"We let her out at the entrance to the building," Liv pointed out. "You didn't know what apartment I lived in. Or what floor I was on, for that matter."

"Your mother called me earlier today and asked me to come over," Sophie told her, her features softening minutely. "She thought you might want to see me."

"I did," Liv said, with a quick squeeze of her hand. "I do."

"Your mother seems like a very nice person, and she obviously loves you a great deal."

"She is a wonderful woman. A bit infuriating at times, but mothers are like that, aren't they?" Liv chuckled, but Sophie's expression hardened again.

"I wouldn't know. I haven't spoken to my mother in twenty years." Sophie looked like she might cry, and Liv quickly handed her a tissue from the end table. It surprised Liv that the usual panic she felt when a woman cried was absent now. She felt nothing but an overwhelming desire to take away Sophie's pain.

"I'm sorry, that was insensitive of me," Liv said when it appeared Sophie had gotten her emotions under control.

"No, please don't ever apologize for having a mother and father who love you." Sophie methodically folded and unfolded the tissue. "Mine didn't even visit me in the hospital. My sister and her family did, and she told my parents about what happened in Walton Creek, but they refused to come."

"All because you told them you were a lesbian?" Liv still couldn't grasp the concept. Parents were supposed to love you no matter what, weren't they? She'd never talked about anything personal with her foster families until the Andrewses. They just wouldn't leave her alone, and she finally came out to them in the juvenile hope they might react the way Sophie's parents had. Much to Liv's surprise, it made them closer, and for the first time in her life she thought she could actually trust someone other than Cindy.

"Yeah," Sophie answered. "Their forty-fifth wedding anniversary is this weekend, and I was planning to show up at the family dinner unannounced. I need closure. The past two decades have passed in a blur. I've finally figured out I can't have a lasting relationship with anyone because I'm afraid they'll abandon me too. When you told Justin nothing was going on between us, I felt like my parents were rejecting me all over again. I just need to know once and for all if I could have salvaged something with them. Then, maybe, I won't wonder if every person that comes into my life will bail on me if something goes wrong."

"I know how you feel." Liv inched a little closer to her, craving the way Sophie made everything in her world feel right. The puppy jumped down and curled up next to Sophie's feet. "Until the Andrews family came into my life, everyone I'd ever known had left me. Starting with my biological parents. I shut down my emotions to deal with all the psychological pain."

Sophie moved closer too, and Liv felt the first twinge of hope that something real was developing between them. "You scare the hell out of me, Agent Kane," she said, her voice almost a whisper.

"I do?" Sophie seemed truly surprised. Liv nodded. "Why?"

"Because you make me feel things I never thought I could. I don't know exactly how you did it, but you've reached a part of me I was convinced didn't exist." Liv watched Sophie's posture finally relax completely. She moved into the touch when Sophie placed a hand on her cheek, her eyes flashing with a desire so obvious it took Liv's breath away. "I *need* you, Sophie. After having you in my life during this case, I can't imagine what it would be like without you now. And honestly, I don't want to find out."

"What are you saying, Liv?" Sophie moved closer, their shoulders almost touching.

"I'm saying I want to spend time with you. I want to date you. I want to get to know you."

"I want to make love with you," Sophie said as her cheeks turned a faint shade of pink.

Liv couldn't stop the smile tugging at her lips.

"Still interrupting me, Sophie? I was about to say that too."

"Maybe you should kiss me so I'll stop talking so much." Sophie closed her eyes and parted her lips slightly when Liv angled her head to do just that.

Liv moaned when her tongue touched Sophie's. Electricity coursed through her body at the feel of Sophie in her arms, and she was certain Sophie felt it too. She pulled Sophie onto her lap so she was straddling her, but then cried out and pulled away from the kiss.

"What's wrong?" Sophie jumped up, her hands out in front of her as if to help her in some way.

"My leg," she said through gritted teeth. The pain shooting throughout her entire leg was enough to kill the mood. She met Sophie's eyes and her disappointment mirrored Sophie's. "Unfortunately, I think the making-love part will have to wait a few days."

"It's okay, honey. I'm not going anywhere."

❖

Two hours later a key in the front door awakened Liv. She lifted her head, relieved to find Sophie still there, stretched out on the couch next to her. She laughed at the smile on her mother's face when she saw them, which woke Sophie up.

"Oh, my God," she said as she sat up quickly and moved away from Liv. Liv felt like she was sixteen again and her parents had just walked in on something they shouldn't have. Sophie stood and started straightening her clothes. "I'm sorry. I didn't mean to fall asleep here."

"Neither did I," Liv said under her breath. Sleeping was the last thing she'd wanted to do when they'd been kissing earlier.

"It's so nice to see you again, Mr. and Mrs. Andrews."

"Please, it's Janet and Kyle," Liv's father said with a grin to match his wife's. Liv finally felt the embarrassment Sophie did when Kim stepped into the apartment as well.

"It's about time," she said with a wink at Liv before heading straight for the kitchen. "Did you tell her you want a stable relationship so I can come live with you?"

Liv wanted to crawl under the couch and hide when Sophie looked at her with surprise. She didn't know what to say, so she simply shrugged and looked to her mother for support. Her mother, however, was trying not to laugh.

"No, Kim, she didn't tell me that," Sophie said before going into the kitchen after her. "Why don't you fill me in?"

"Dad, how do you put up with women?" Liv asked when her parents sat down on either side of her on the couch.

"Most of the time it's not easy," he said with a chuckle. "But believe me—when all is said and done, it's well worth any angst you might have to deal with."

Liv smiled, because she knew deep down he was referring to when she'd first come to live with them. He put his arm around her to hug her.

"We're going back to Chicago the day after tomorrow," her mother said.

Liv sat up straight again and looked at her, anxiety making her heart race.

"Relax. Kim has promised to keep an eye on you, and I'm sure Sophie won't mind helping out too. Your father needs to get back for an important meeting. He's going to be chief of staff at the hospital."

"What?" She grabbed his hand and held it tight. "That's fantastic, Dad. I'm so proud of you."

"We're both very proud of you too, Olivia," he said with a grin. He looked toward the kitchen before leaning closer and speaking quietly. "Hang on to this one with both hands, would you? She's definitely a keeper."

"I know, and I don't intend to let her get away."

"We should be heading to bed, Janet," Liv's father said after they'd visited with Sophie for a while. Sophie couldn't believe they'd been sitting there talking for almost two hours. She glanced at Liv, who looked exhausted. "We're happy to see you feeling better, Sophie. It's a pleasure to meet the woman who seems to have captured Olivia's heart."

"Dad," Liv said, her tone playful.

"Will we see you in the morning?" Janet asked before they headed down the hallway to the guest bedroom.

Sophie's cheeks warmed and she was at a complete loss as to how to respond.

Liv answered for her.

"Yes, you will."

"Wonderful," Kyle said as he led his wife out of the living room.

"Well, that was embarrassing," Sophie said when they were finally alone again.

"Really?" Liv asked seriously. "They like you a lot, you know."

"That doesn't mean they want me to be spending the night here with you." Her breath caught at the pure desire on Liv's face. "Fuck, Liv, you've got to stop looking at me like that."

"Why?"

"Because I'm not sure I can keep my hands off you, and you need some sleep. Not to mention the pain your leg is giving you."

"Sleep is overrated." She smiled, and if Sophie had been standing, her knees would have given out. Liv hadn't smiled much since they'd met, and really, who could blame her? But God, that smile was lethal. "Besides that, I slept more than enough while I was in the hospital for three very long and extremely boring days."

"I am not having sex with you while your parents are sleeping in the next room," Sophie said adamantly. Liv sighed dramatically and Sophie couldn't help but laugh.

"I had no idea you were such a prude, Sophie Kane."

"A prude? Are you telling me you would do that?"

"God, no, but it's a good thing they're going back to Chicago the day after tomorrow," Liv told her. "You have to stay the night, though. I told them you'd be here in the morning."

"I'll sleep on the couch."

"Oh, goody, 'cause that's where I'm sleeping too." Liv rubbed her hands together and Sophie shook her head with a grin.

"I'll sleep in your bed then," Sophie said. Liv opened her mouth, but Sophie put a hand up. "And no, you can't change your mind and tell me you're sleeping there too."

"You're no fun."

"I can be all kinds of fun, just not when parents are close by." Sophie's heart sped up when Liv met her gaze. "Damn it, Liv, I told you to stop looking at me like that."

"I can't help it." Liv grabbed Sophie by the shirtfront with both hands and pulled her on top of her as she stretched out on the couch. Sophie was careful not to jar Liv's leg, and she couldn't stifle her moan when their pelvises pressed together, their lips mere centimeters apart.

"You're not making things easy for me, Andrews." She sounded needy, and she didn't care. All that mattered was how Liv's body felt underneath hers. And how much better it would feel without their clothes in the way.

"It's not in my job description to make things easy for you, Kane," Liv said before she closed the gap between them, covering Sophie's mouth with her own. Sophie felt the wetness between her own legs when Liv moaned into her mouth, her hands cupping Sophie's ass and pulling them even closer together.

She intended to pull away. But when Liv's tongue touched her lips, asking for entry, Sophie lost all sense of her surroundings. She complied, parting her lips and deepening the kiss as the excitement began to build. The slide of Liv's tongue along her own caused an involuntary thrust of her hips, her body searching for release. Liv gasped and turned her head away from Sophie.

"Watch the leg," she said with a wince.

"It serves you right for trying to seduce me on your couch with your parents not more than twenty-five feet away." Sophie carefully pulled away from Liv, making sure not to hurt her again. "Do you need anything? A pain pill maybe?"

"There's only one thing I need," she said with a salacious grin.

"You're incorrigible."

"Good night, Sophie."

"Good night." Sophie made her way to the master bedroom, her legs shaking badly. How in the world could Liv get her so worked up with a simple make-out session on the couch? Sophie liked Janet and Kyle Andrews, but she couldn't wait for them to return home.

CHAPTER THIRTY

Sophie sat watching Liv sleep with the puppy curled up and his head on her arm, and for some reason, the sight contented her. Janet and Kyle had left to return to Chicago earlier that day, and Sophie came to check on Liv after she finished work. She was thoroughly convinced she would be happy as a hostage negotiator and was really looking forward to completing the training and getting on with the new chapter in her life. One she hoped Olivia Andrews would be a part of.

"What time is it?" Liv mumbled as she opened her eyes and looked around the living room. "Christ, what day is it? I feel like I've been sleeping for weeks."

"It's Thursday, and it's almost seven o'clock in the evening," Sophie said. She got up from her chair and eased onto the couch next to Liv, closing her eyes and letting out a sigh when Liv's hand snaked under her shirt to touch her back. She had spent most of the day at Liv's apartment the day before, but went home so Liv could spend the last evening with her parents before they left. The level of familiarity they'd developed was strange because they really didn't know each other very well. It also comforted Sophie to realize she could have that kind of intimacy with another woman. After a moment she stole a look at Liv. "How much longer until your leg's healed enough for some exercise?"

"What kind of exercise did you have in mind?"

"A nice cardio workout would be good, don't you think? Get the heart pumping and the blood racing." She laughed when Liv groaned and pulled her hand away. Sophie kissed her on the cheek. "I brought dinner. Are you hungry?"

"Starving."

"You didn't answer my other question."

"My leg?" Liv asked. Sophie nodded. "I'm thinking probably Saturday night after your parents' anniversary dinner."

"I've decided not to go, Liv," she said. Liv looked at her strangely, and Sophie avoided eye contact as she helped her get up off the couch. She'd thought about it a lot over the past couple of days and decided she didn't need to put herself through the hell of confronting them. If they ever wanted to get in touch with her, Barb could give them her number.

"You need to, Sophie." Liv's tone was stern, and Sophie finally looked at her.

"Is that right? Is this how it's going to be? You telling me what to do?" She was half joking, and she smiled to soften her words.

"No, I'll never tell you what to do, baby, but I think you need to see them. It'll be good for you to show them what they've missed all these years."

Sophie put a hand on Liv's cheek and felt a wave of desire when Liv covered it with her own and placed a kiss in the center of her palm. They hadn't done any more than kiss, and it was driving her crazy. She wanted Liv's hands all over her body, and she was getting restless waiting for that to happen.

"I don't need them, Liv," Sophie said quietly. "I have Barb, and her husband and kids. And now I have you. I've done all right without my parents for the past twenty years."

Liv looked uncomfortable as she turned her head away and started to reach for her cane. Sophie grabbed it for her and held it out.

"What's wrong? Are you going to be sick?"

"I don't know. I mean, I don't want to push you. But damn, family is everything, you know? I don't think you should give up on them, that's all."

"I promise to think it about it, okay? It might be time for me to move on and accept that I'm okay without them. But if you feel that strongly about it, I'll consider it. Okay?"

Liv smiled and brushed a strand of hair away from Sophie's face. "Good enough. I just want you to be happy, baby."

Sophie kissed her softly, letting her lips linger teasingly just out of reach for a moment. "You make me happier than I ever thought I could be."

❖

"You really need to give this little guy a name," Liv said as she offered him a tiny piece of pizza crust. "I can't keep calling him *puppy* all the time."

"Do you want him?" Sophie asked. Liv looked at her and thought about it. It would be nice to have a dog to come home to, but it wasn't any more responsible of her to have a dog than it was to have Kim live with her.

"I don't think I should."

"Your parents told me about the dog you had when you were younger." Sophie stopped eating and sat back in her chair. "They thought you might like it."

"I would like it, but it's not realistic," Liv said, scratching behind his ears. "When I went to live with them, they had a five-year-old golden retriever. We fell in love with each other and were inseparable until I left for my training at Quantico. I'd love to have a dog, but I'm gone too much."

"Kim wouldn't mind taking care of him, and I could come over to walk him a couple times a day when you're out working a case."

Liv smiled and looked at the dog, who was staring at her, waiting for her to give him another tasty morsel.

"I was thinking of Nathan for a name."

Liv's heart clenched at the mention of Victor's last name, and she met Sophie's eyes.

"You really know how to work me, don't you?" She looked at the dog again, trying not to let Sophie see how touched she was. "Fine. Nathan, would you like to live here with me?"

He wagged his tail and let out a tiny bark in response. That settled, they started eating again in silence.

"So, Kim wants to live with you," Sophie said, phrasing it as a statement rather than a question. Liv didn't know what to say.

"She's been asking for months, and I keep telling her a single FBI agent who's rarely home is not the ideal foster parent for her or anyone else." Liv sat back in the dining-room chair and dropped her slice on the paper plate in front of her.

"What do *you* want, Liv?"

"I'd love to be able to give her a stable and loving home like I was given," Liv said, hoping like hell their current conversation wouldn't ruin their budding relationship. "I can't do it though. Not with the career I have."

"What's wrong with the home Mary's given her? Isn't she a loving parent?"

"Mary's got her hands full with the other three, and as a result, Kim gets pushed aside sometimes," Liv said. "A lot, actually."

"What's wrong with them?" Sophie asked. Liv hadn't had the time to introduce Sophie to Mary and her other kids, so Sophie really knew nothing about Kim's current situation, other than the fact Kim wanted so desperately to live with her.

"Brad is nine," Liv said after a moment. "His parents were killed in the car accident that left him a paraplegic. He spends so much time with doctors and psychiatrists it's a wonder he's ever outside of a hospital. He has every reason in the world to be angry, but he's the happiest kid I know. The twins are four. Their mother abandoned them on some church stairs when she found out they both had leukemia. Mary took them all in without hesitation, and I honestly don't think she's ever regretted her decisions. She's a nurse, so she's a bit better equipped to deal with their medical needs than most people."

"Does Kim have medical problems?"

"No, unless you want to count her rather surly attitude with most people." Liv smiled with affection and shook her head. "She was the first one to come live with Mary, and she's been there just over a year."

"What if your situation were to change? What if you could take her in?" Sophie asked, her expression thoughtful.

"What do you mean?"

"Look, I realize we haven't known each other long, and there's no way to tell where things might go between us," Sophie said quietly. "I mean, we haven't even gone on a date yet."

Liv held her gaze and found hope bubbling to the surface of her heart. She'd never even considered a long-term relationship with anyone, and here she was hoping that was what Sophie wanted. Sophie truly completed her and made her feel alive for the first time. It was as if she could see everything clearer than before. Sophie was exactly what had been missing in her life.

"Go on," Liv prodded her, when Sophie paused as though she was unsure what Liv's reaction would be. Liv reached across the table and covered Sophie's hand with her own.

"I've always wanted to have a child. I never wanted to do it on my own, but I kept holding out hope I'd meet the right woman some day." Sophie stared at their joined hands as she spoke. "If things were to work out between us, would you consider bringing Kim into our home? Once I'm done with my training, I'll be working at the office in Philly for the majority of the time. I'd only have to travel to places where they needed a negotiator. I wouldn't be gone for days at a time, most likely. I could be here for her when you're out in the field. I mean, I know I'm being awfully presumptuous, but you'll notice I said *if* things work out—"

"Kane, you talk too much." She squeezed Sophie's hand gently and smiled when Sophie finally looked at her. Liv stood and pulled Sophie up with her. When Liv's arms went around her waist, Sophie draped her arms around her shoulders. "I think it's wonderful you want to give Kim a stable home. And it means a lot to me for you to throw that out there so soon. At least I know where you stand. A teenage foster kid could be a deal breaker for most people. I'd hate to invest time in a relationship with you just to find out six months down the road you don't want kids."

"Andrews, has anybody ever told *you* that you talk too much?" Sophie was looking at her with a serious expression, and Liv had to laugh.

"No, I have to admit I've never had that problem before. I've always been the strong, silent type."

"Don't get me wrong, I really like it when you talk, but right now, I need for you to shut up and kiss me." Sophie nipped at Liv's lower lip, and Liv groaned in response as she pulled Sophie's body flush against hers. "I need you to touch me, Liv."

Liv leaned down to kiss her, and her knees quivered when Sophie's tongue slid alongside hers. She held her tighter, worried if she let go Sophie might simply disappear. Nothing in her life had ever felt so good—so *right*. Liv sighed with contentment when Sophie's hand moved up her neck and tangled in her hair. She whimpered when Sophie broke the kiss.

"I want you naked. Now."

"I thought you wanted to wait until Saturday." Sophie grinned, then turned serious as she took a step back and looked down at Liv's leg. "Are you sure you're all right for this kind of physical activity?"

"Sophie, if I have to wait any longer I might explode. This incessant throbbing between my legs *really* needs to stop soon." Liv pulled her close again and closed her eyes when Sophie rested her head against her shoulder. "Your kisses drive me crazy."

"I could say the same about you," Sophie murmured against her neck before kissing her there. "I dream about you, Liv. I dream about all the things I want to do to you, and the things I want you to do to me."

"Show me," Liv whispered as arousal swept through her body.

Without a word, Sophie took her by the hand and led her down the hallway. She stopped right outside the door and turned to look at Liv, her expression serious.

"You're sure you want this? I don't want any regrets."

"I could never regret making love with you, Sophie." She was surprised to realize she meant it. Sophie's eyes softened at her words, and she turned to enter the bedroom.

Sophie slowly removed her clothing, Liv's pulse quickening when Sophie pulled down the zipper on her pants. She stared, hoping to God she wasn't salivating, because she was well aware of her mouth hanging open. She'd die if she didn't get her hands on Sophie in the next few minutes.

"Maybe you should get naked too," Sophie told her, stretching out on Liv's bed with just her panties and bra on. Liv quickly stripped down to her boxers and sports bra before lying down next to her. Her eyes were stuck on Sophie's cleavage, and she didn't tear them away until Sophie placed a finger under her chin and forced her eyes upward. "You aren't naked. I want you naked."

"You wanted me naked *too*," Liv said with a devilish grin. "In order to be naked *too*, I believe you need to be naked first."

Liv unclasped Sophie's bra, and as she slipped the straps down her shoulders, she watched Sophie's eyes close. Sophie sighed in pleasure when her breasts were exposed and Liv took one taut nipple in her mouth. Sophie put a hand on Liv's shoulder and tried to push her onto her back, but Liv's cry of pain stopped her.

"Shit, I'm sorry," Sophie said. She gently touched the large angry bruise there. "Does it hurt a lot?"

"Not as much as my leg does," Liv admitted, once again staring at the firm breasts before her. She forced herself to meet Sophie's eyes and shrugged. "But neither of them hurt so much that I don't want to continue. If you want me on my back, just tell me."

"I want you on your back," Sophie said breathlessly. Liv rolled over and held her breath when Sophie moved above her. Instead of settling in, Sophie moved down to slide Liv's boxers off. Liv managed to get her sports bra off while Sophie shed her own panties, then didn't have much time to think before Sophie was on top of her. Liv spread her legs to allow her room, and Sophie gently thrust her hips. "You feel so damn good, Liv."

"I need you, Sophie. I've never needed or wanted anyone more. I was a fool to try to deny it." Liv moved her hands to Sophie's hips and pulled her snug against her pelvis. "You're so fucking beautiful."

"Sweet talker," Sophie said before raining kisses down on Liv's lips and neck. She straddled Liv's good leg and pressed herself hard against the muscular thigh. "Oh, God, I think I might come before you ever touch me."

"We can't have that, can we?" Liv moved her right hand between their bodies and groaned when her fingers found Sophie's molten center. The sound deep in Liv's chest caused an involuntary spasm in Sophie's abdomen. "Jesus, you're so wet."

"It's all for you, Liv," Sophie whispered, moving back up to kiss her ear. "I'm going to come for you."

Liv could tell she was close, and even though she wanted to take it slow and easy, Sophie needed it fast right now. Liv easily slid two fingers inside her, and Sophie bucked against her hand.

"Fast is okay this time, baby, but next time, we're doing it at my pace," Liv said, loving the way Sophie moved against her when she began circling her clit with her thumb. Sophie spasmed around her fingers and Liv turned her head so she could kiss her, swallowing Sophie's screams as she came. When Sophie finally relaxed into her, Liv slowly withdrew her fingers and then held her close.

"I'm sorry." Sophie laughed with obvious embarrassment. "I feel so needy right now."

"Don't ever be sorry for needing release, baby," Liv told her, tightening her arms around her. "It's sexy as hell that you just go after what you want."

Sophie raised herself on her elbows and met Liv's eyes. A part of her thought she was crazy, but she felt a pull to Liv, so strong it was almost like a magnet. It was way too soon, but she was almost certain she was falling in love with Olivia. She prayed Liv felt at least a little bit like she did.

"What do *you* want, Liv?" Sophie slowly traced a circle around Liv's nipple, watching it harden under her touch.

"I want endless days like this, Sophie."

It wasn't really what Sophie had been looking for, but she knew it wasn't easy for Liv to admit needing anything from anyone. She shifted so she was propped up on an elbow looking down at Liv, and her heart broke when she saw a tear running down her cheek. Liv tried to wipe it away quickly, and Sophie decided it was best to not mention it.

"When Kraft had you in his house, I realized I'd finally found a woman who meant more to me than the job. All that mattered was getting you out of there alive."

"Is that why you risked your own life?" Sophie choked back her own tears, not quite knowing how to react. It was unfathomable that anyone could even consider putting their own life on the line for her. She'd thought her parents would have at one time, but that fantasy had been completely shattered, and she never thought she'd find that kind of devotion again. She was sure that would be something missing from her life forever. When she touched Liv's face, just to make sure she was real and not imaginary, Liv clasped her fingers and kissed them.

"You're an amazing and beautiful woman, Sophie Kane. I only met you a few weeks ago, yet I can't imagine not having you in my life," Liv told her. "You've made me realize I *am* capable of loving another human being, and that means more to me than I can say."

"Did you just say you love me?" Sophie asked with a grin. Liv closed her eyes and turned her head away from her, but Sophie wasn't about to let her put those walls up again. She gently squeezed a nipple between her thumb and index finger until Liv looked at her again. "Please don't shut me out, Liv. You need to talk about your feelings."

"I do love you, Sophie," Liv said after a moment. "I've never been in love before, but there's no doubt in my heart that's what I'm feeling now. And just so you know—I've *never* said those words to anyone else."

"I love you too, Liv." Sophie felt light-headed at the admission. It was more than she'd dared to hope for. A tear ran down her cheek, and Liv used her tongue to wipe it away. "I think we're both talking too much now, don't you? I want you to come for me."

"Yes," Liv said. "I want that too."

Sophie moved between Liv's legs, careful to avoid the gunshot wound in her thigh. Liv threaded her fingers through Sophie's hair, guiding her head to a nipple that Sophie covered with her mouth. Liv moaned when Sophie made her way lower, her tongue leaving a trail from Liv's breast to the apex between her thighs.

Liv's scent was intoxicating, and Sophie didn't hesitate before taking her clit into her mouth. Liv held her close with a hand on the back of her head, and Sophie sucked her gently at first, but with more fervor when Liv began to move frantically beneath her. When Sophie slid two fingers inside of her, Liv cried out and Sophie immediately felt the contractions begin around her fingers. Liv begged her to stop after a few moments, and Sophie crawled back up the bed to lie next to her.

"You're fucking amazing."

"I could stay here in your bed forever with you and be perfectly happy." Sophie rested her head on Liv's good shoulder and allowed Liv to hold her.

"That sounds nice, but I think we'd have to get up to eat once in a while."

"I suppose. If we have to."

"Sophie, what are you going to do now that the case is over?"

Sophie raised her head to look at Liv. The uncertainty in those eyes made her heart ache. Liv was obviously still worried about being involved with a coworker.

"You know I've already gone back to my hostage-negotiating training. My assignment to your team was temporary. We won't be working together, Liv. At least not directly."

Liv smiled, and Sophie settled in against her once more. The soothing rhythm of Liv's heartbeat quickly lulled her to sleep.

CHAPTER THIRTY-ONE

Sophie awoke the next morning to the aroma of bacon cooking. She stretched her tired muscles and smiled at the memories of what exactly had caused the soreness. She turned over and pulled Liv's pillow close, inhaling the musky scent of her that lingered, and sighed with utter contentment. She was drifting off again when she heard Liv come into the room. Sophie opened her eyes in time to see a golden blur jump up beside her and wag a tail happily as it stuck its nose in her face.

"Good morning, beautiful," Liv said.

Sophie looked over and her breath caught when she saw Liv standing in the doorway, her hair wet and a smile taking over her features. It was a good look for Liv, and Sophie hoped she'd be seeing it quite a bit in the future.

"Good morning," Sophie said with a grin.

"I'd bring you breakfast in bed, but it's a little hard to carry a tray full of food when one hand's occupied with this damned cane." Liv hobbled more than she had in the past couple of days. Sophie saw the grimace of pain Liv tried to hide as she scooted over to make room for her.

"Is it bothering you a lot?" Sophie moved the cotton shorts Liv had on so she could get a look at the wound.

"Only because of what we did last night, and trust me, I'm not going to complain," Liv said as she put a hand over Sophie's and stopped her doctoring attempt.

"Does Nathan need to go out?"

"He peed on the newspaper in the kitchen sometime overnight, so I'm sure he'll be fine until we get around to taking him out."

"Is anything going to burn, or can I just stay here in your arms for a few minutes?" Sophie didn't wait for an answer but snuggled in close to Liv, her head on Liv's shoulder, and made an unintelligible sound when Liv held her tight.

"Breakfast is done cooking, but if we stay here too long the eggs will get rubbery and the bacon will be cold," Liv said, her hand slowly running the length of Sophie's arm and stopping when their fingers entwined.

"I don't care," Sophie whispered. "I don't care if I never get to eat again as long as I can spend the day in bed with you."

Liv didn't respond, and after a moment Sophie raised her head to look at her. She was watching Nathan as he curled up at the foot of the bed and looked like she was deep in thought. Sophie cupped Liv's jaw in her hand and turned her head.

"What's wrong?"

"I've just been thinking about you going to your parents' anniversary party," Liv said quietly. She turned her head and kissed Sophie's palm before smiling. "I don't want you to go if you really don't want to."

"Why the change of heart?" Liv shrugged and directed her attention to the puppy once again. "Hey, Liv, don't do this. Please don't shut me out. Last night you really wanted me to go, so tell me what you're thinking."

Liv stared straight ahead, not looking at her. She gave Liv the time she needed to figure it out in her own head, and when Liv finally met her eyes, her heart broke at the tear rolling down her cheek. What had it cost Liv to let her see this vulnerable side of her? Liv closed her eyes momentarily when Sophie wiped the tear away with a thumb.

"Family's important, Sophie," she said, her voice obviously strained, but she never looked away. "And if there's any chance they could have changed their opinion about you and your life, I think you should try to establish contact. Maybe they just don't know how to mend the relationship, and you making the first step might be all it takes."

"Baby, I know how important family is to you after what happened to you growing up. I'm so happy the Andrews family found you." Sophie had hoped in the past what Liv was saying was true, but she knew deep down it wasn't. Her father would never have anything to do with her again, but she didn't know how to articulate that fact to Liv. "Things were said that can never be taken back. When I came out to them, I expected them to be disappointed. All my mother ever talked about was me getting married and giving her grandchildren. I guess Barb being pregnant at the time wasn't enough for her. I told them one day after we got home from church."

Sophie stopped for a moment because she hadn't expected to get emotional, but she cleared her throat and refused to let the tears that threatened fall. She gave a rueful smile and went on, glad Liv waited patiently rather than feeling a need to fill the silence.

"My father backhanded me. He'd never hit me before. In fact, I was always Daddy's little girl, so when he did that, it scared the hell out of me. He grabbed me by the arm and tried to drag me out to the car, telling me he was taking me right back to the church so our priest could get rid of the demon inside me. Of course I refused, and the only way to get him to stop was to kick him between the legs. To this day it's a blur, and I don't remember much of it, but I do remember that." Sophie paused and looked down at Nathan, who had his head on his paws and was watching her as though he understood every word she was saying. "He dropped like he'd been shot, but he never quit yelling obscenities at me. My mother did nothing to stop it, and they kicked me out of the house right then and there. I couldn't even go up to my room to get any of my things."

"I'm so sorry you had to go through that, Sophie." Liv's voice was a strangled whisper, and Sophie saw another tear in the corner of her eye. "You never talked to them again after that day?"

"Oh, I did." Sophie nodded. "Barb and her husband Jay never hesitated to let me come live with them, and I'll always love them for that. Who knows what might have happened to me if they'd shunned me too? Anyway, when I was accepted to start my training at Quantico, I called them, assuming they'd be proud of what I was doing. You know what they did?"

"I can't begin to imagine."

"They hung up on me. Then they called Barb at work and suggested she should explain to me what it meant to be disowned." Sophie saw the anger flash in Liv's eyes before she looked away. Sophie knew she was biting her tongue, that what Liv really wanted to do was make her parents pay for how badly they'd treated her. All the more reason to let it go, as far as Sophie was concerned. "I tried a few times over the years to contact them until they changed their phone number about ten years ago and left strict orders with Barb to never give it to me." Sophie caressed Liv's stomach, her thoughts clearly in the past. "Before this case I'd convinced myself I needed to try one last time to reconcile, but I've come to terms with it, Liv. There's nothing left to salvage. If they want to get in touch with me, they can do it through Barb. I'm done with them."

Liv stared into her eyes so intently Sophie had to fight the urge not to flinch. After a moment, Liv kissed her on the lips.

"Move in with me," she said, her voice almost a whisper.

"Excuse me?" Sophie pulled away and sat up, letting the covers fall to her waist, which exposed her chest. She smiled when Liv's eyes dropped, focusing on her breasts for a quick moment before meeting her gaze again.

"Shit, did I say that out loud?" Liv smiled, and caressed a nipple with her thumb.

"Yes, you did," Sophie laughed as she pulled Liv's hand away and brought it to her lips.

"I love you, Sophie, and we could take this slow, see where it leads, but I know what I want. I want to be your family. I'm off for the next few weeks, so we can spend a lot of time getting to know each other. If we can make it that long without killing each other, then perhaps we could talk about having Kim come live with us too." Liv finally stopped to take a breath. "Maybe we might even consider adopting her."

Sophie stared at her, suddenly aware of her heart beating incredibly fast, and she really had no clue what to say in response.

She finally nodded and Liv smiled before kissing her again. She let Liv push her onto her back, and when the kiss ended, Sophie opened her eyes to see Liv gazing at her with pure, undisguised love.

"I love you, Sophie," she said, making Sophie's heart swell.

"I love you too."

"Okay, now that we have everything settled, I think Nathan will understand if I want a few more minutes with my girlfriend before he totally disrupts our day."

Sophie slid her arms around Liv's neck and pulled her into an embrace. *Girlfriend.* She could definitely get used to that.

About the Author

PJ Trebelhorn was born and raised in the greater metropolitan area of Portland, Oregon. Her love of sports—mainly baseball and ice hockey—was fueled in part by her father's interests. She likes to brag about the fact that her uncle managed the Milwaukee Brewers for five years, and the Chicago Cubs for one year.

PJ now resides in western New York with Cheryl, her partner of many years, and their menagerie of pets—six cats and one very neurotic dog. When not writing or reading, PJ spends her time rooting for the Flyers, Phillies, and Eagles, or watching movies.

Books Available from Bold Strokes Books

Slingshot by Carsen Taite. Bounty hunter Luca Bennett takes on a seemingly simple job for defense attorney Ronnie Moreno, but the job quickly turns complicated and dangerous, as does her attraction to the elusive Ronnie Moreno. (978-1-60282-666-3)

Touch Me Gently by D. Jackson Leigh. Secrets have always meant heartbreak and banishment to Salem Lacey until she meets the beautiful and mysterious Knox Bolander and learns some secrets are necessary. (978-1-60282-667-0)

Missing by P.J. Trebelhorn. FBI agent Olivia Andrews knows exactly what she wants out of life, but then she's forced to rethink everything when she meets fellow agent Sophie Kane while investigating a child abduction. (978-1-60282-668-7)

Sweat: Gay Jock Erotica edited by Todd Gregory. Sizzling tales of smoking-hot sex with the athletic studs everyone fantasizes about. (978-1-60282-669-4)

The Marrying Kind by Ken O'Neill. Just when successful wedding planner Adam More decides to protest inequality by quitting the business and boycotting marriage entirely, his only sibling announces her engagement. (978-1-60282-670-0)

Dark Wings Descending by Lesley Davis. What if the demons you face in life are real? Chicago detective Rafe Douglas is about to find out. (978-1-60282-660-1)

sunfall by Nell Stark and Trinity Tam. The final installment of the everafter series. Valentine Darrow and Alexa Newland work to rebuild their relationship even as they find themselves at the heart of the struggle that will determine a new world order for vampires and wereshifters. (978-1-60282-661-8)

Mission of Desire by Terri Richards. Nicole Kennedy finds herself in Africa at the center of an international conspiracy and being rescued by beautiful but arrogant government agent Kira Anthony, but is Kira someone Nicole can trust or is she blinded by desire? (978-1-60282-662-5)

Boys of Summer edited by Steve Berman. Stories of young love and adventure, when the sky's ceiling is a bright blue marvel, when another boy's laughter at the beach can distract from dull summer jobs. (978-1-60282-663-2)

The Locket and the Flintlock by Rebecca S. Buck. When Regency gentlewoman Lucia Foxe is robbed on the highway, will the masked outlaw who stole Lucia's precious locket also claim her heart? (978-1-60282-664-9)

Calendar Boys by Logan Zachary. A man a month will keep you excited year round. (978-1-60282-665-6)

Burgundy Betrayal by Sheri Lewis Wohl. Park Ranger Kara Lynch has no idea she's a witch until dead bodies begin to pile up in her park, forcing her to turn to beautiful and sexy shape-shifter Camille Black Wolf for help in stopping a rogue werewolf. (978-1-60282-654-0)

LoveLife by Rachel Spangler. When Joey Lang unintentionally becomes a client of life coach Elaine Raitt, the relationship becomes complicated as they develop feelings that make them question their purpose in love and life. (978-1-60282-655-7)

The Fling by Rebekah Weatherspoon. When the ultimate fantasy of a one-night stand with her trainer, Oksana Gorinkov, suddenly turns into more, reality show producer Annie Collins opens her life to a new type of love she's never imagined. (978-1-60282-656-4)

Ill Will by J.M. Redmann. New Orleans PI Micky Knight must untangle a twisted web of healthcare fraud that leads to murder—and puts those closest to her most at risk. (978-1-60282-657-1)

Buccaneer Island by J.P. Beausejour. In the rough world of Caribbean piracy, a man is what he makes of himself—or what a stronger man makes of him. (978-1-60282-658-8)

Twelve O'Clock Tales by Felice Picano. The fourth collection of short fiction by legendary novelist and memoirist Felice Picano. Thirteen dark tales that will thrill and disturb, discomfort and titillate, enthrall and leave you wondering. (978-1-60282-659-5)

Words to Die By by William Holden. Sixteen answers to the question: What causes a mind to curdle? (978-1-60282-653-3)

Tyger, Tyger, Burning Bright by Justine Saracen. Love does not conquer all, but when all of Europe is on fire, it's better than going to hell alone. (978-1-60282-652-6)

Night Hunt by L.L. Raand. When dormant powers ignite, the wolf Were pack is thrown into violent upheaval, and Sylvan's pregnant mate is at the center of the turmoil. A Midnight Hunters novel. (978-1-60282-647-2)